WHEN WE DANCE

A WALTZ WITH DESTINY: BOOK TWO

ALANNA LUCAS

ISBN 978-1-956367-04-1

Sebastiani Press

PO Box 1234

Simi Valley, Ca 93062

Cover by Dar Albert

❀ Created with Vellum

For Nono

CHAPTER 1

*I*t was supposed to be a glorious day, the happiest day of her life. The day she had dreamt about ever since she was a child when all her hopes and dreams would come true. Instead, it was becoming Artemisia's worst nightmare. She had been waiting anxiously for over an hour at the church.

Perhaps he's met with some ill fate?

She fanned herself, pacing the width of the vestibule. The swish of her wedding dress on the stone floor mocked her with each step she took. She could only hope that he *had* met with some ill fate. Shaking her head, she sighed into the quiet space of the corridor. That was an unkind thought, indeed. Better to reserve her anger if… no, when Mr. Chartwick arrived.

It was rare for her to give into these sorts of musings. But she could not help it, not today at least, and especially not when Nigel was near.

Peering through the aisle door into the church, she spied *him*. Nigel Rochefort, the bane of her existence ever since her debut five years ago. He sat in the second to last pew at the rear of the church, inclined at an angle, full of self-confidence, one leg stretched out in front of him, barring passage to anyone who might want to sit in his row. The smug look she could see on his face made her body tense and heartbeat quicken.

"Oh, where is Mr. Chartwick?" she muttered under her breath.

The Honorable Mr. Chartwick was *never* late. Perhaps he would arrive soon, and they *would* be married and live in the country raising a brood of children. It was her fondest desire to marry and have a family of her own. She'd never imagined in her wildest dreams that it would ever happen to her. Although she had a large dowry, no gentlemen had ever paid her much attention. She was too… different.

Unlike her blonde sisters, she had dark auburn hair and an olive complexion, resembling her Italian grandmother. Only her crystal blue eyes were like her father's. Whereas they complemented his fair complexion, on her, they were far too dramatic and intense.

She had ceased looking in the mirror five years ago after a disastrous first season.

She remembered the whispers as if it were yesterday. *With skin as dark as hers, she will never make a match… And those eyes, they are too disturbing by half… She is far too plump and looks dreadful in pink… She is so uncoordinated, two left feet…* The insults went on, and no matter what she did, how hard she tried, she could not dismiss them, the worst coming from Nigel, who'd once been her friend.

It had been the last official ball of her first season. Artemisia had clung to the hope that someone—anyone— would ask her to dance, complement her, offer a kind word… anything. Instead, it had been the worst night of her life.

Lord Owens had asked her to dance, only to regret it

moments later when she'd stepped on his toes. He'd cried out so loudly with pain that the couples near to them had stopped mid-step, causing others to bump into them. Within a matter of moments, the entire ballroom had been filled with laughter.

However, the sound had not covered the harsh words of those around her. *She simply has no grace… Such a horrible dancer… Poor Lord Owens, his foot must be crushed…*

Lord Owens had left her standing alone.

Blurred faces and spiteful words had swirled about her. She recalled running from the room in tears, trying to find a peaceful, secluded corner to regain her composure. When she'd emerged onto the dim veranda, she'd heard the deep, rumbling laughter of several of the *ton's* most notorious rakes.

"You really played it up, Owens, old boy!" a young dandy had exclaimed, slapping Lord Owens on the back. *"Did you see the look on her face when you asked her to dance? It was like she had never been asked before."*

"She probably hadn't. She is the worst dancer the ton has ever seen, even worse than Miss Greaves."

It was at that moment that the not-so-Honorable Nigel Rochefort had decided to add his two pence. *"At least Miss Greaves is pretty."* The rest of the rakes had cheered at that comment.

Lord Owens had chimed in, adding further insult to injury, "Her *skin is absolute perfection, milky-white…"*

Artemisia had not been able to take the insults any longer. In a daze of anger, she'd stormed through the crowded ball-room toward the entrance hall. Once clear of the crush, she had not stopped, not even when she was safely home inside Germayne House. Upon reaching the sanctity of her room, she'd looked in the mirror, and all she'd seen was a misfit. All she'd heard were the insults and laughter reverberating through her mind. She'd ripped the blanket off the bed and thrown it over the mirror.

That distant night was the last time she'd looked at her reflection. Ever since then, she'd put complete trust in her maid to make her look as presentable as possible. Whenever temptation arose to glance at herself, she remembered those hurtful words and knew she was better off not knowing.

But when Mr. Chartwick had begun courting her several months ago, all her past woes had faded under the guise of finally being able to realize her dream to be married. It was a practical courtship, no flowery sentiments, or heated embraces. He was a perfect gentleman. Even after he proposed, Chartwick never pressed his advantage or tried anything untoward. She was so elated over the prospect of being married and having a home of her own, she did not stop to wonder *why* there were no heated embraces or stolen kisses. Perhaps if she had, she would not be standing alone, waiting for the groom on her wedding day.

A gentle hand on her shoulder brought her back into the present. She did not know which memory of this day would prove to be more painful over the coming years—being abandoned at the altar, or the look of sympathy in her mother and father's eyes.

Squeezing her shoulder, her father gently began, "My dear, I do not believe Mr. Chartwick intends to make an appearance today."

His words were lost in the sea of emotion that boiled within as hot tears threatened to spill. Her hopes were shattered. What was she to do? How would she endure the gossip?

"I will make an announcement." Father placed his hand on the small of her back, guiding her toward the exterior double doors. Placing a soft kiss on her forehead, he whispered, "Go on home with your mother."

Artemisia watched him enter the church filled with guests, his head held high in the face of yet another scandal. All eyes turned his way in anticipation of an explanation. When he passed the second to the last pew, a confident blond head turned round, his gaze meeting Artemisia's. The self-righteousness in Nigel's stare inflamed her agony. He shrugged one elegantly clad shoulder and gave her a lopsided, scornful sneer of a smile that said, *I told you so.*

In that moment, all of her excellent manners deserted her.

Instead of leaving the church and finding comfort in the bosom of her family, instead of remaining calm, Artemisia sealed her fate as a hot-tempered spinster. Walking with determination, she went along the nave and approached Nigel. He did not stand, nor speak a word, just continued to smirk at her.

The muscles in her hand tightened into a fist with an ache that screamed for release. She stared down at his perfect square jaw, focusing on her target. Ignoring common sense, she swung her arm with all her might.

When her fist hit his firm chin, she stifled a cry of pain. Pursing her lips, she sucked in a deep breath, blinked away the tears, and stormed out of the church, grabbing her bouquet of pink roses from her shocked mother. Instead of leaving to the sound of cheerful bells pealing, gasps and laughter were her wedding march.

SHE'D ACTUALLY STRUCK HIM.

Nigel could not believe what had just happened. A woman had just hit him. Not just any woman or casual acquaintance, but Artemisia. Not a delicate slap, but a hard punch full of pent-up anger. That had never happened to him before. He just sat there… stunned.

Did she suspect?

Before he had the opportunity to reflect further on the question, her father, Lord Germayne, made an announcement and swarms of guests brushed past him, giving him curious looks as they filed out of the church. His first thought was to stay put and wait for everyone to leave. He was in no mood for inquisitive gossipmongers, but there again, he did not want to become trapped by those very same gossips.

Following the herd of bright dresses and fanciful hats out of the church, whispered theories swirled around him as to the whereabouts of Mr. Chartwick. The general consensus was that the groom had cold feet. Nigel knew otherwise.

He was within earshot when Lady Lamden began to weave one of her vicious tales. "…and this is not the only scandal facing Lord and Lady Germayne. Did you notice that Miss Philippa Germayne was not in attendance?"

She and her fellow rumormonger stopped walking and huddled together, too deep in tittle-tattle to notice that anyone was eavesdropping.

Casually standing behind a large urn of flowers, Nigel strained to hear the conversation.

"I have it on the best authority that the young lady in question is not indisposed, but has disappeared altogether."

"Disappeared?"

"She has not been seen since yesterday when she was discovered alone in the park with a certain notorious rake."

Nigel's stomach lurched with guilt. *He* was the notorious rake they spoke of. Although he had done nothing wrong, had only tried to comfort a friend in need, his past scandals could very well ruin Philippa's future.

The whispers lowered. He leaned in, trying to make out

what the two scandalmongers were discussing. The scent of hothouse roses tickled his nostrils. Before he could gain control of his senses, he let out a large sneeze, his hands pushing the urn off its pedestal.

The pristine white porcelain vessel flew through the air, crashing onto the floor and breaking into dozens of pieces, spraying water on those nearby. Startled screams sounded around him. When at last he regained his composure, he was met by the formidable stare of Lady Lamden, whose dress had suffered from the unfortunate accident.

"Trouble seems to follow wherever you are, Mr. Rochefort." The sourness in Lady Lamden's voice was even more annoying than the lady herself.

Flicking his gaze upwards, he let out a heavy breath. He was in no mood to deal with Lady Lamden. His tone was laced with sarcasm. "I have no clue what you are referring to." Bowing his head in farewell to the ladies, he uttered a firm, "Good day."

CHAPTER 2

The sun shone high in the sky, mocking Artemisia's failure. She should have been married now and enjoying the company of family and friends at her wedding breakfast. Instead, she sat alone in her room, staring out the window with a heavy heart, and wondering how her life had taken such a miserable turn. She smoothed the front of her cream silk gown, admiring the embossed pale pink roses adorning its hem. Pulling the pins out of her hair with force, she released her once elegant coiffure. The bouquet of pink roses that her mother had given her was now shredded and spread across the floor, the light scent of blossoms drifting through the room, taunting her with what was not to be.

Her mind raced with all the possibilities as to why Chartwick had left her to be sacrificed to the *ton's* vicious tongues. No matter how hard she tried, she could not discern his motives. He'd always been pleasant and respectful toward her, and they'd seemed to get on well together.

There'd been only one problem. Despite the pleasantness, there was no passion, no spark. Artemisia's mother had been unwilling to discuss such matters, and told her that, with time, greater affection would come. Even Harriet, her elder married sister, had refused to entertain the topic. So, Artemisia had given no further thought to that drawback, until today.

The one and only kiss they had shared had been an utter disaster. It had happened on the day Chartwick proposed. Artemisia remembered thinking that he had the look of a man who was being led to the guillotine. She should have listened to the alarm that had resounded in her head. There were no flowery declarations of undying love, just a practical proposal, after which he'd stated: "I suppose I should kiss you now."

Unsure of what to do, she'd closed her eyes and leaned in, just as Chartwick leaned in too, their heads knocking together with a clunk. Chartwick had smiled with embarrassment, given her one firm, brief kiss on her lips, raised his head, and then left the room without further words. That should have been her first indication that they truly were not suited for each other. However, her elation over knowing that she would not be a spinster had overruled her normal good instinct.

What would her future be now? Collapsing on the soft feather pillow, she covered her eyes with her arm. Her head ached from all the emotions she'd experienced over the last twenty-four hours. Not only had she been humiliated in the worst conceivable way for a woman of her station, but she was also keeping her youngest sister's secret.

Not for the first time in her life, she found herself covering for Philippa, allowing her own wants to drift into a hazy background.

It had all begun only yesterday when Philippa had stormed into her room, begging for her help. Artemisia should have questioned her sister further, should have convinced her to take a different course. But when she saw the glee in Philippa's eyes, she'd known without a doubt that her sister's mind was made up, and she would proceed with or without Artemisia's help.

"But you will miss my wedding," Artemisia remembered saying, trying to hide her hurt.

"You will be so busy with your guests that you will hardly know if I am present or not." Philippa took Artemisia's hand in hers. "Please understand. I want to be happy… like you."

Artemisia had not been happy at that moment, or in the days leading up to her wedding. For reasons she could not explain, she had been quite out of sorts as of late. When she mentioned her concerns to her mother, she was told they were just bridal nerves, and it was normal to have such emotions.

Philippa had been relentless in her quest. "This is my only chance to be happy. I don't want to be a spinster. And besides, Mother and Father will be so preoccupied with the wedding that they won't think to come after me right away."

With each pleading word, Artemisia's guilt rose. "I doubt…"

"Please Arte, I need you. Mr. Keates *is* my one, my only. Don't you find him a pleasant fellow?"

Artemisia did like Mr. Keates. But that was not the issue. The obstacle was Mr. Keates' profession. He was the son of the head stableman. Both she and her sister knew that their prospective parents would never approve of such a match. Tears had begun to stream down Philippa's face in a deluge, and hiccupping on her sobs, she'd not stopped her pleading. "Please… please, you must help me. I love him."

In that moment, Artemisia could not deny her sister anything, setting her current woes in motion.

She would never forget the look of anguish on her parents' faces when they'd stormed into her room, only a couple of hours before her wedding that would never be, waving her sister's cryptic note.

Dear Father and Mother,

I've gone to follow my heart. I will return home before too long. Do not worry.

Philippa

"What do you know about this, Artemisia?" her father had demanded as he waved the letter fervently. "And do not tell me you had no knowledge of this. Philippa tells you everything."

Artemisia had stood speechless.

Her heart was torn in two as she'd watched her mother reach out and place a trembling hand on Father's arm, her eyes filled with tears, her words laced with worry and sadness. "What are we to do?"

"If anyone can discover Philippa's whereabouts, it is Weston," her father had stated with certainty. He'd turned his gaze on Artemisia. "Until we receive word, we will carry on as if nothing is awry."

The mention of Weston had boded ill for Artemisia. His skills as an investigator were unparalleled, and she had no doubt that he would discover what Philippa had done. And when that happened, her parents would discover her involvement as well. Her only consolation at that moment was that, by the time her parents discovered Philippa's elopement, she would be married and on her honeymoon.

Her mind flitted to the last words Philippa had declared once she'd agreed to her scheme. "You will have your Mr. Chartwick, and I will have my Mr. Keates. We will both be married to the men we love."

The words had stung Artemisia's bruised heart.

The men we love.

That was the problem. Artemisia realized that she'd never

been in love with Mr. Chartwick. She had only accepted his proposal because everyone had commented on what a splendid match it was. Not to mention that he was the only person to have ever asked. At three and twenty, her prospects appeared to be nonexistent.

She feared growing old, alone and unloved.

Bolting upright into a sitting position, she glanced around the room at the discarded slippers and gloves, the shredded flowers, and the hairpins on the floor. She whispered her confession into the stillness. "I don't love Chartwick. I never have. I have no affection for him whatsoever."

Was she so desperate to marry and have a family of her own that she was willing to enter into a sacred union with someone she did not love?

Images of her parents and how much they still cared for each other came to the forefront of her mind. She remembered the tales her *Nona* had told her as a child about everlasting love. She wanted more than just a marriage of convenience. She wanted more than to just *be* married.

She wanted a happy ever after filled with passion and love.

The realization was both liberating and frightening. She still did not know what her future would hold, but in the midst of her anguish, she did discover one thing. She would marry for love, or not at all. With that firm decision in mind, she decided it was time to tell her parents of her desire and hoped they would understand.

With her chin held high and prepared for battle, she opened her bedroom door and walked with purpose down the deserted hall. The soft rug under her bare feet was a sinful luxury. She could not remember the last time she'd left her room with her toilette in such a state of disrepair, but she cared naught for who might see her. Her mind was made up, and she was not going to tarry one moment longer.

But then she stopped short. Something seemed odd. Not one single servant was about. The house was as silent as a grave. It was as if all its occupants were in mourning. Before she could ponder this strange occurrence, a chambermaid exited one of the other bedrooms. Their eyes met for only an instant, and Artemisia detested the pity that flashed in the young girl's gaze before she dropped a quick curtsey, then turned and scurried away in the opposite direction. Artemisia's spirits sank even lower; this was how so many would view her from now on.

Shaking off the desire to run straight back into her room and never emerge, she swallowed hard and proceeded towards her destination.

Running a trembling hand along the smooth wooden rail, she was halfway down the grand staircase when a determined knock sounded on the front door.

"Curious old gossipmongers," she spat under her breath, thankful that no one was around to hear her. "Why won't they just let me be?"

She watched the butler perform his duties with the same *de rigueur* he used to tackle all his tasks. A stream of bright light cascaded across the black-and-white checkered marble floor as he opened the door, and the silhouette of a larger-than-life man intruded into her home. Glancing up, she saw the bane of her existence once more.

What is he doing here? her mind screamed with anger and hurt.

"I must speak with Miss Germayne." His voice was just as firm as his knock had been.

"I am sorry to inform you that Miss Germayne is not receiving visitors at this time…."

Artemisia did not wait to hear the last part of Cuthbert's standard speech to unwanted visitors. Gripping the newel post, she tried to control her anger. She would not take her frustrations out on the butler, but would save her words for the man who'd just invaded *her* domain.

"It is quite alright, Cuthbert. I will speak to Mr. Rochefort."

Cuthbert closed the door and eyed the intruder with disdain. Under normal conditions, the very composed servant would have hidden all emotion, but today was anything but normal. He had obviously heard every last detail of her humiliation below stairs.

She descended the last few steps, coming face to face with the man who had caused her such grief over the last few years.

Courage, do not fail me now.

"This way, Mr. Rochefort." Her voice sounded cold even to her own ears. *Good.*

Nigel followed Artemisia into the opulent day parlor. Sunlight filtered into the sparsely furnished white and gold room. The serene air about her matched the elegant interior. How could anyone ever believe this woman dull?

He only meant to soften her resolve, not anger her further, when he blurted out, "You look lovely." As soon as the words left his mouth, he regretted them. She stared at him as if he'd just informed her that she looked like a troll just emerged from under a bridge. If looks could kill, he would definitely be lying dead on the expensive, opulent rug.

"Don't patronize me." Her words were harsh, uncaring. "Why are you here?"

He did not know where to begin. The storm of emotions

brewing inside was muddling what he wanted, and should say. How was he to convey his concern for her sister after what he had done?

"I understand your sister is unwell."

Alarm streaked across her face, if only for a brief moment. She quickly schooled her features before inquiring, "What have you heard?"

He attempted nonchalance, but was certain he'd failed. "Only that she is unwell."

She gave him a sideways glance and raised a delicate brow in question. "Nothing more?"

Artemisia was hiding something, he was sure of it. With an unslippered foot, she stroked the elegant carpet. He watched, mesmerized by the delicate motion. Thoughts of what was hidden beneath the layers of silk entered his mind. He wanted to run his hand up her smooth, delicate leg and—

"What is it you desire?" Her stern question brought him out of his delicious musings.

You.

Damn, where had that thought come from? Clearing his throat, he uttered the first appropriate thing that came to mind, "Simply to inquire after your family's well-being."

"My family's well-being, Mr. Rochefort?" Her voice got louder with each word.

They were back to formalities. Although they had known each other their entire lives, this is what their friendship has been reduced to, and he had no one to blame but himself. If only she understood.

"You are concerned about someone other than yourself?" Artemisia huffed, giving him an incredulous look. "I do not believe it."

"It's just that I overheard Lady Lamden…" He pursed his lips. He should not have mentioned *that* gossipmonger.

Crossing her arms, Artemisia shook her head. "It is just as I thought." She paced back and forth before turning an angry gaze on him. "I know Philippa met you in the park, and yet you come here claiming to be concerned for my family, when what you are really concerned with is the gossip surrounding your name."

"I *am* concerned about your family."

He genuinely was.

Lord and Lady Germayne were good friends of his mother's, and their neighbor in London. He would never wish ill upon any of them.

Only to dash Artemisia's hopes and dreams.

Damn his conscience for reminding him.

Artemisia's crystal blue eyes darkened several shades, and her face was flushed with rage. When she finally spoke, she was practically shouting at him. "How do you think my family fares? My sister is unwell, I was left at the altar and humiliated in front of the *ton*, and all you can think of is yourself. You are the most selfish individual I have—"

"I am *not*."

"You can add childish to the list of attributes," she scolded with sarcasm.

Childish? How could she think he was childish? He opened his mouth to protest but was interrupted by the appearance of Artemisia's mother.

Lady Germayne dashed into the room. "I heard shouting from all the way down the hall."

She was similar in height to Artemisia, possessed the same shade of auburn hair, but that was where the resemblance ended. But, despite the differences, mother and daughter made a striking pair.

"It is nothing, Mother. Mr. Rochefort was just leaving."

Nigel took the hint. He would find a more suitable time to

speak with Artemisia. He bowed to Lady Germayne. "If there is any way I may be of service, please do not hesitate. I am only a house away."

"You are far too kind," Lady Germayne said with a sincere smile.

Nigel turned to take his leave, but not before hearing Artemisia mumble under her breath with sarcasm. "Yes, *far* too kind."

CHAPTER 3

Shuffling down the steps of Germayne House, Nigel's spirits plummeted while the guilt that had been festering in his stomach toiled and churned. His meeting with Artemisia had not gone well. What had he expected? His appearance yesterday in the park with her sister had fueled the rumors about Philippa's current whereabouts, not to mention that he had single-handedly ruined Artemisia's wedding.

Shaking his head, he reminded himself that he'd *had* to stop the wedding. Chartwick was not in love with Artemisia. And besides, the two would have never suited. Chartwick was much too dry and humorless, and not nearly man enough for Artemisia.

She needed someone who would make her laugh, challenge her mind, who loved and adored her. She deserved nothing less.

The short walk to Monfort House did not improve his mood. For a brief moment, he contemplated going for a ride in the park, but it was nearing four o'clock. He would not be late.

Walking up the front steps, the door before him opened like clockwork. "Good afternoon, sir. Your mother is waiting in her parlor." Fergusson's tone and mannerism were as restrained as ever. If the butler had heard any of the rumors, his countenance revealed nothing.

"Thank you, I will go to her straight away." Afternoon tea with his mother had become a daily ritual since his father's passing, and the favorite part of his day when they were in residence together.

His footfall sounded on the white marble floor, announcing his arrival. Attempting to hide the ill effects of the day from his mother, he pasted a big smile onto his face. "Good afternoon, Mother." He bent down and kissed her soft cheek. The sweet scent of lilac that she always wore had been a soothing balm since childhood, enveloping his senses and relaxing his jumbled nerves.

He was half-way to his seat when his mother abruptly asked, "I take it you've heard all about the poor Germayne girls?"

Damn. A vein in his neck pulsated instantly with renewed tension. The gossips had wasted no time circulating the news. Lowering himself onto the well-cushioned chair, he tried his hand at nonchalance. "Girls?"

"Don't try to feign ignorance to me. I know you better than that, Nigel." The stern scowl on his mother's face reminded him of when he was a young lad and constantly pushing the boundaries of propriety. Sucking in his breath, he was about to argue when Mother softened her tone and asked with concern. "What happened?"

"With regard to…?"

She closed her eyes and let out a long, deep sigh. When she opened her eyes, her countenance was calm once again. "We will start with Philippa. Is it true that you met with her alone in the park yesterday? And do not lie to me, dear boy."

Nigel might be a lot of things, but dishonest he was not, especially when it came to his mother. "I *was* in the park yesterday and happened across Philippa. She had been crying, and I comforted her." When his mama raised a skeptical brow in question, he quickly added, "Nothing more."

"Why was she so upset?"

"She wouldn't say exactly, only that she had decisions to make." He stopped, trying to remember what Philippa had divulged between sobs, but nothing about their conversation had made any sense to him. "I assumed she was crying over some lad and told her to follow her heart."

"How romantic of you," his mother responded with sarcasm.

Leaning back in his chair, he took a sip of tea, looked at her, and combated her sarcasm with some of his own. "I thought so, too." He saw pain flashing deep within her eyes. Guilt punched him in his gut. He did not mean to cause her distress.

Mother's voice quavered. "I suppose you have not heard the rumors that are now circulating because of your romantic nature?"

Whenever the gossipmongers sunk their teeth into him, his mother was always the one to suffer. She often proclaimed she could not believe that either of her sons would embroil themselves in the scandalous activities that were being circulated as tittle-tattle by the *ton*. She had always held fast to the notion that her boys would never tarnish the Monfort title.

Of course, his elder brother, Ranulph, never did anything to incur attention. He had always taken his responsibility as the heir to the earldom to the utmost extreme.

Nigel had tried to adhere to a similar philosophy at one

point in his life, but nothing he'd ever done had seemed to please his father. After years of trying to make the man proud of him, he'd simply given up and indulged himself in the darker entertainments Town had to offer.

However, now that his father was dead, his notorious rakish pastimes had lost their luster. Something had changed for him of late. He found himself wanting to live up to his mother's expectations. He wanted to be known for more than his scandalous lifestyle.

When he did not respond, Mother elucidated on what she had heard. "It is rumored that the poor girl is on her deathbed, beside herself with grief over your refusal. There are others who have suggested that she ran away to the country to escape all the rumors. And then there is poor Artemisia—"

"What about her?" His quick response and defensive tone caused Mother to raise her brows in question.

Narrowing her eyes and tilting her head to one side, her words came slowly and with emphasis. "What have *you* done?"

Nigel was about to say 'Nothing' but felt his mama's scrutinizing gaze. "I could not let her marry him."

Chartwick was one of Nigel's oldest friends. Only days earlier, he had confided over a bottle of whisky that he was only marrying Miss Germayne for her dowry and that he was in love with another. Despite Chartwick's dire need to clear his father's debts, Nigel had encouraged his friend to run off with the woman he claimed was the love of his life. With Chartwick, one never quite knew. He was always falling in and out of love with some female. Except for Artemisia. Chartwick maintained he felt only friendship for her. That was the only excuse Nigel had needed to sabotage the wedding. He had convinced himself that he was doing

Chartwick a favor, but the festering sensation in his gut told him otherwise.

His mother just stared at him in silence, waiting for his reply. The problem was, he did not know why he'd done what he had. He gave her the same excuse he had been giving himself since he discovered Chartwick's lack of amorous affection for Artemisia. "Chartwick is in love with another."

"And that was reason enough for you to interfere with their wedding? Did Chartwick ask for your assistance?"

Deep brown eyes waited in question. Over the last year and a half, he'd watched them fill with more and more sorrow. He could not look at Mother without seeing the grief that had been consuming her since the loss of her husband... his father.

Nigel knew without a doubt the constant arguments and broils that had dominated his relationship with his father had taken their toll on his mother's well-being. Whenever she was placed in the middle of one of their arguments, she would never choose sides, and often withdrew. Her melancholy would last for days until Nigel and his father feigned reconciliation.

Even on his deathbed, his father had not managed a kind word for his younger son. When Lord Montfort had finally succumbed, all Nigel felt was relief. He had not mourned the man, but instead, mourned for his mother's loss. Only once had Mother confided *her* greatest regret—that Nigel had not made peace with his sire.

Nigel glanced at his mother. Her eyes continued to bore into his soul. He could not stand to cause her more grief.

"No, he did not." Nervous energy streamed through his body. Teeth clenched, he rubbed his jaw. Standing up, he stormed to the open window and braced his hands on the sill. He could see leaves shimmering in the sunlight, feel the gentle breeze that moved through the garden and filtered into the parlor, carrying with it the sweet scent of roses in bloom. The world outside was peaceful, content. A direct contrast to the inner distress and anxiety he was currently experiencing.

His mother sat there without a word, waiting for him to elaborate.

"No, he did not," he repeated, his voice just above a whisper. He turned away from the window to face his mother. Rubbing his jaw once more, he continued with his justifications. "He and Artemisia would have made each other miserable. He was only marrying her for her dowry. Chartwick deserved more."

Fingering a rose-colored napkin on the table, his mother questioned in a tone that bespoke a hidden purpose. "Chartwick or… Artemisia?" She worried her bottom lip for just a moment before speaking a truth that struck to his very core. "I know you, Nigel, perhaps better than you know yourself at times. You demand honesty from those around you, and yet, you cannot be honest with yourself. You cannot seem to admit that perhaps Artemisia means more to you than—"

"Mother, it is nothing like that. A friend was in need, and I decided—"

"—to sabotage that poor girl's wedding," she finished his sentence with a knowing smile.

How had he let his life get so out of control? Three days ago, his biggest problem had been choosing a new mistress. Two evenings ago, his friend had confided his worries. Yesterday, he'd set into motion Chartwick's escape from entering into a loveless marriage, and told a young woman— who was now missing—to follow her heart. In the process, he had hurt Artemisia.

Perhaps he should not offer any more advice.

His mother stood and then approached him. "My dear

boy, you need to ask yourself why you did what you did."
Her deep brown eyes held the wisdom of years of experience.
As much as he didn't want to admit it, her words were true
and wise. "For as long as I can recall, whenever you returned
from visiting Marcus at Knollwood, the first word out of your
mouth was 'Artemisia'." She placed her hand over his heart.
"Follow *your* heart." She patted his chest, and then walked
away with that same wise smile on her face.

Nigel stood there, dumbfounded. *His heart…*

BY THE TIME the sun had set, London was abuzz with the
scandal of Philippa's disappearance and Artemisia's abandonment at the altar. There was even speculation that Philippa
had run off with Chartwick. It was most humiliating. And
then there was Nigel's inconsiderate, unkind, and unthinkable
appearance earlier that afternoon. His feigned concern for her
family had left a sour taste in her mouth. No sooner had he
departed than she'd retreated to her room without
explanation.

Artemisia knew she could not avoid her parents for long.
Although she had wanted to speak with them, Nigel's visit
had ruffled her senses. She needed time to recover, or she
would never be able to say the words that were eating her up
inside.

Hours later, her time of reckoning arrived.

She swallowed hard as she entered her father's study. The
warm glow from the fireplace cast eerie shadows across the
walls, increasing the uneasiness of her desperate situation.
She was not looking forward to having this conversation.

Her chest tightened, and her voice wavered as she
muttered the words, "You wanted to see me?"

Her parents were sitting side by side on a deep burgundy settee. She knew their cozy appearance was just a façade for what lay beneath. Her father spoke first. "Your mother and I have been discussing the latest scandals to affect our family."

Sadly, this was not the first time the Germayne family had had to endure embarrassment. It was just last year that, yet another rumor had raced throughout the *ton* that Artemisia was not, in fact, the daughter of Viscount Germayne, but of an Italian actor. Rumors had long circulated about Artemisia's "true" father. The fact that she looked nothing like her father, or her two sisters for that matter, didn't help.

The first time Artemisia heard whispers about her illegitimacy, she was only seven years old. She was devastated. She kept the emotions bottled up for days until her father finally convinced her to confide in him.

"Without a doubt you are my daughter," she remembered him saying. "Your mother and I are as much in love now as on the first day we met." After that, she'd never doubted her paternity. But, unfortunately, other causes of insecurity had surfaced.

Now, just when Artemisia thought she was finished with scandal, another one had been laid at her doorstep. She regretted her decision to aid her sister. In hindsight, she should have marched Philippa straight to their parents, avoiding all entanglement.

Mother took up where Father had left off. "We are curious about the countless coincidences surrounding Philippa's absence, Mr. Chartwick's disappearance this morning, the arrival of Mr. Rochefort this afternoon, and the rumors…"

"…which all come back to Nigel Rochefort. Care to explain?" Father ended her mother's speech with concern in his voice and a raised eyebrow. His crystal blue eyes were most unsettling.

Artemisia did not know what to say. She wanted to tell them the truth, but Philippa had sworn her to secrecy. Twice. Earlier, she had skirted the issue with a watered-down excuse, then again, on the way to the church. What more could she say without betraying her sister?

Her parents sat unnaturally still, waiting for her response regarding Nigel. At least, about this she could answer with all honesty. "I do not know what his involvement is."

Mother frowned, confusion and distress clear in her voice. "But you struck him?"

Artemisia sighed. She did not know why she'd done what she had—only that she was furious, humiliated, and… hurt. Even just the thought of Nigel made her blood boil. But that response would earn her the same lecture she had always received about decorum. *Proper young ladies control their emotions. Proper young ladies would not strike anyone.* She was tired of being a proper young lady and always trying to control her emotions, when all she really wanted to do was be herself.

Patting the seat beside him, her father commanded in a gentle tone, "Come and sit with us." When she approached, he took her hand in his and squeezed lightly. "We are both in agreement that the country is a safer location for someone in your situation."

"At least until the gossip dies down, dearest," her mother added.

What exactly *was* her position? Because of what had happened, was she now unworthy of another chance at matrimony? Would she be forced to settle for someone else she did not love if she were ever to marry? Now that she realized that she wanted love, not just a good match, she did not want to settle. How long would she have to stay in seclusion? The questions whirled and collided in her mind.

Her mother stroked her arm, her words tender and caring. "Do not worry, my love. A visit to Knollwood will cheer you. And besides, Aunt Lou was expecting you and Char..." Mother stopped short, apparently realizing Artemisia would not want to hear the name, once again, of the man who'd caused her pain, then cleared her throat and continued, "I see no reason why she would not be agreeable to having an extended visit from her favorite niece."

Knollwood *was* Artemisia's most favorite place in the whole of England. Over the years, she had visited her aunt often and the two had formed a unique bond. Their minds were so similar. Artemisia always felt much more herself at Knollwood than in any other place.

"I think I would very much enjoy a visit to see Aunt Lou." It would lift her spirits, and she'd be in the perfect place to allow the gossip to die down. This interview with her parents was turning out better than expected.

"Good," her mother started before she eyed her father.

Then again...

The tone in her mother's voice suggested this was the brief calm before the storm. "Now that is settled, we must discuss your sister."

Swallowing hard, Artemisia fumbled with the words, "Is... is something the matter with Harry?"

"Harriet is fine. Her confinement is progressing—"

"We are speaking of Philippa." Father had interrupted her mother. That was never a good sign.

Artemisia kept her gaze downcast, showing tremendous interest in the floral-patterned rug. The seconds drew out. She raised her eyes and met her father's stern stare.

"Artemisia." His tone rumbled to her core. "Tell us where she has gone."

"I...I do not kn...know exactly." It wasn't really a lie. She did not know every stop along Mr. Keates and Philippa's journey north to Gretna Green. She was just omitting the destination.

Out of the corner of her eye, she saw her mother pat Father's hand, as if begging him to hold his tongue, before she spoke. "How are we to help her if we do not know what has become of her?"

Philippa's cryptic note this morning had made the situation much worse. Artemisia had made a promise to her sister, but equally, she did not want to deceive her parents. *Why must life be so difficult?* There must be a way to appease both parties.

The questions came in rapid succession from her mother. "What did she say upon her return from her walk yesterday? Did she leave *you* a note? Did she have a lover's quarrel with Mr. Rochefort?"

"Mr. Rochefort? Good heavens, no." Artemisia jumped off the settee and paced back and forth in front of the fireplace, her heart racing at the thought of Nigel. She turned to face her parents. "Why would you think that?"

"Miss Jerome sent word that your sister was seen yesterday in the company of Mr. Rochefort and was crying." There was a long pause before her mother began speaking again. This time, her tone was softer. "And after what you did at the church this morning, it seems only natural that he has some involvement."

Nigel, Nigel, Nigel. Everything in her life always came back to that… that scoundrel. A simple plan to help her sister find happiness had exploded, leaving *her* to clean up the shattered pieces, as always.

"Is that what everyone is saying?"

"I'm afraid so, my dear. Why *did* you…?" Her mother could not even say the words.

"I struck him because…" The tears she had been controlling streamed down her cheeks as she began sobbing heavily. "I don't know… because… he is just a horrible person and… and…" Somewhere deep in her soul, her heart answered, *because a long time ago you thought you loved him and he did not return the sentiment.*

"Oh, my dear, don't cry." Mother rushed to her side and wrapped her arms about her. Artemisia instantly felt the love in her mother's embrace. Her body relaxed and her breathing eased. "It will all turn out for the best." Her mother stroked the dampness from her face. "Please, tell us why Philippa would run away and not come to us."

Once again, Artemisia was torn. She did not want to betray her sister, but nor did she wish to dishonor her parents. She could see the pain in her mother's eyes. She did not want to cause her or Father further grief. When she'd agreed to keep Philippa's secret, it had been with the knowledge that, after her wedding, she was to travel with her new husband to his country estate, and so would not be subjugated to such an inquisition. Philippa had promised to explain everything in the note she was to leave for their parents. But instead of comforting them, her note only raised more questions. However, this was not the first time Philippa had put her in an awkward situation.

No matter what she said, she was about to betray someone she loved. Taking a deep breath, she hiccuped a sob, and offered only part of what she knew. She let out a heavy sigh. "She… she went to discover herself… in the country."

Her father threw his hands in the air. "What is that supposed to mean?"

Artemisia flinched at his angry words. "Please, Father, don't be angry," she whispered out. "It is not my secret to tell. I promised her…."

His voice rumbled, "Why do you always cover for her?"

Father was irate, and it was all her fault. The seconds ticked on for what felt like an eternity, waiting for his next words. When he finally spoke, his tone was hushed and filled with sorrow, a direct contrast to a few moments ago. "I just want to know that she is safe." Never in her life had she seen him so discomposed.

She detested her role in this game of charades and deceit. With a dullness in her chest, she answered her father. "She is safe."

He cleared his throat numerous times before he dissemi-nated how the family would proceed. "We will wait to receive word from Weston. Until then, we will continue to make it known that Philippa is indisposed, and that you have accompanied her to the country to convalesce. If she corresponds with you, you are to send word immediately." His glare brooked no argument, his words were firm and clear.

"Yes, Father."

THE TURN of events surrounding her wedding day had taken its toll on Artemisia. After supper, which was spent mostly in silence, she excused herself and went straight to her room.

In its solitude, she could ponder those most puzzling questions that had been plaguing her throughout the day. What was wrong with her? Why was she not good enough for Chartwick?

Only the man in question could answer the latter, but the former was something she had much more control over. She knew she could not dance, despite hours of lessons. It had been a couple of years since the last instructor. Perhaps she should subject herself to another session of torturous tutoring and pray that she'd magically improved.

And then there was her skin, which was too dark by the *ton's* standards. It had been five years since she'd last looked at her reflection. What would she see now? For one breath of a moment, she contemplated taking the cloth off the mirror to discover what horrors would be revealed, but then thought better of it. Nothing had ever been accomplished by dwelling on what could not be changed. No, it was best that she accepted the facts and retreated.

After she opened the French doors that led out onto the small balcony, cool evening air filtered into her room. Her nightly ablutions brought some comfort, too. Picking up her favorite hairbrush, she strolled outside.

The stone beneath her unclad feet was cold and soothing. Mist had started to roll in, creating an air of mystery and suspense in the garden below. Brushing her long auburn hair, she sang her favorite Italian love song that her *Nona* had taught her. How she missed her grandmother. Nona would have known what she should do. "Believe in yourself, *la mia piccolina.*" Nona's words echoed in her mind.

Tomorrow, she would leave for Knollwood. Perhaps she would find what her soul desired there.

THE HOUR WAS LATE. Under normal circumstances Nigel would have gone to his club, or a gaming hell, but he was too consumed with guilt over his recent innocent actions. Well, only one action had been innocent. Sabotaging Artemisia's wedding had been very much intentional. The question remained, why exactly had he done it?

Too restless to sleep, he escaped to the quiet sanctuary of

the garden. He was contemplating his mother's words when a beautiful voice called to him through the rolling mist. He was like a sailor being lured to his doom by the sound of a siren beckoning him into the depths of the great ocean blue.

Following the sound, he moved through the mist, his mind cloudy with impressions of an auburn-haired beauty with eyes like the sea, reclined on the rocks. He reached the edge of the lawn and still the voice continued to call to him.

Taking advantage of a neighboring tree, he climbed his way up the sturdy trunk. When he neared the top, he paused, relishing in the sweet sound. Brushing the leaves to one side, in the distance beyond, the source of the beautiful voice was revealed to him.

The sight that met his eyes was most alluring. A deep longing called from within and coursed through his body like lightning, leaving him excited and bewildered, and more confused than ever, all in the same breath.

When did life become so complicated?

CHAPTER 4

*L*ondon was still abed as the early morning sun fought against the haze to make its presence known. Even the birds had more sense than to be about in such dreariness, Artemisia thought as she wrapped her cloak about her, warding off the chill. Her parents had decided it was best that she depart early, before the gossipmongers came to life, to embark on the full day's journey to Knollwood. She hoped to spend most of the time sleeping. The days leading up to her wedding, followed by her sister's elopement, and then the scandals that had followed, had taken their toll on her countenance. Not to mention that she was anxious to hear from Philippa.

Once the journey began, however, her mind would not rest. Any thought of sleep flew out the window and vanished in the mist as she pondered her future. She could not help but wonder if she would ever find happiness, if someone would love her for who she was.

The sound of a gentle snore disturbed her thoughts. She glanced over to the opposite corner of the carriage, where her maid, Maggie, was sleeping peacefully. "At least one of us will be rested."

Glancing out of the window at the passing countryside, her mind once again drifted, only this time to the man who had humiliated her in front of her family and close friends. Although Chartwick's father had reassured Artemisia's family that his son would pay a heavy price for his actions, and that the matter of his whereabouts was being investigated, she had yet to receive a single word from her fiancé... *former fiancé*, she supposed. She did not know if he'd met with some accident, or was hiding in the country, or had left England altogether to avoid marrying her. As much as she detested what he had done to her, the rumors being circulated about the Germayne family were far worse.

Philippa's disappearance, speculation over her parents' 'troubled' marriage, reports of Chartwick's infidelity, her unfortunate response to Nigel's smug expression on her wedding day, and his brief visit to her home were all talk of the *ton*. The only consolation was that Nigel had not reappeared on her doorstep.

At least her escape from London also meant escaping him.

Nigel. A heavy sigh pressed against her chest. Why was he the bane of her existence? Why couldn't he just let her alone? Why...

Sounds of the city drifted away. She watched as London sank into the horizon and with it, its unpleasant smells and the hustle and bustle of town. She breathed in the crisp air of the countryside. With each posting inn they passed, the excitement of being at Knollwood grew.

There, she could heal. There, she could hide from vicious tongues.

Hours later, the carriage turned onto Knollwood's well-maintained drive, the endless grounds unfolding before them. When the grand manor finally came into view, the weight of her world lightened, and a sense of safety washed over her.

Knollwood was a magnificent medieval creation. Lush green lawns and immaculate flowerbeds framed the length of the front exterior, the outer walls of wood and stone concealing its vast depth. Three courtyards, which could only be seen from the vast expanse of interior facing windows in each wing, divided the property into tidy sections.

When the carriage came to a halt, an efficient footman prepared the steps, opened the door, then assisted Artemisia as she descended. The air was beginning to cool with the approach of evening, and with it, a hint of newly blossomed roses lingering on its wings. She twirled round, enjoying the beauty all around her. There was no haze. There was no traffic or the sounds of people scurrying about. Only the peaceful rustling of leaves in the wind and the distant sound of horses neighing could be heard. She felt… at home.

"Arte!" She turned around in time to see her plump aunt descend the front steps of the house in a flurry of yellow silk, her white wavy hair escaping her lace cap. "You've come at last." She ran up to Artemisia and gave her a firm hug. She looked around as if her niece had lost something before asking, "Where is this new husband of yours? I regret I was not able to attend…."

"There was no wedding." Artemisia's statement was dry and flat.

"What…?" her aunt started to ask, but instead pulled Artemisia towards the house. "Come inside, freshen yourself after your long journey, and then we will dine in the Green Parlor and you can tell me all about what did not happen."

THE ODDLY NAMED Green Parlor was, in fact, not green but pink. It was not a place for men with all its frilly doilies and cushions. No, it was most definitely a sanctuary for ladies. Beautiful floral paintings hung on the walls, adding to the impression of a delicate environment.

The truth was, Aunt Lou did not even care for the color pink. But it kept the men in her life at a distance. The cleverly decorated room was *her* hideaway. Neither Aunt Lou's late husband, nor his nephew Marcus, the current Marquess of Hawthorne, had ever set one foot in this room. Both had claimed it was too feminine, too frilly, and far too pink.

Artemisia settled onto an oversized damask chair, kicked off her shoes, then tucked her feet beneath the folds of her paisley evening dress.

Her aunt did not stand on protocol when it was just the two of them. The evenings were often informal, dining here, in the Green Parlor, and reading aloud or working at embroidery. There was never any demand to appear to be anything that you were not. Artemisia loved being here with her aunt. Lou was the one person in the entire world who understood her plight.

Aunt Louella—Lou to her family—had never been considered a beauty. When she'd married her late husband, it was with the understanding that she was to provide an heir. Once her duty was done, they would have no use for each other and could live in separate residences, so long as appearances were maintained.

Unfortunately, Aunt Lou had been unable to carry a baby to term, and so, had not provided her husband with what he desired most. Toward the end of his life, with no regard for Louella's feelings, he'd sought comfort in imbibing spirits to the point of drunkenness while in the arms of multiple mistresses. When the old Marquess died, his title had passed to his nephew, Marcus. Although Marcus was seven years her senior, Artemisia had spent much time with him over the years. He was the brother she'd never had.

She had always wondered how her aunt managed to maintain her dignity, find joy in the everyday, and rise above the horrible rumormongers. When questioned, Aunt Lou's simple response always was, "Life is too short to be miserable."

Closing her eyes, Artemisia's own plight came into focus. She'd never been one to put her own wants and desires ahead of her sisters'. She had always been there for both Harriet and Philippa, solving their problems and covering for them after some escapade. She'd never had her own escapade or adventure, and now…

A loud sigh escaped her lips. What would her future hold?

"Tired from your journey, Arte?"

Opening her eyes, she responded, "Not at all." Her aunt's tender gaze warmed her heart and soothed her soul. She loved her parents with all her heart, but she and Aunt Lou were kindred spirits.

"Good. We have much to discuss. I want to hear all the news from London."

The following couple of hours were spent deep in conversation. Artemisia told her aunt all that had occurred—or rather had not occurred—and her unladylike behavior in the church towards Nigel. Aunt Lou was well acquainted with him. He and her nephew were good friends, and Nigel had often spent summers at Knollwood with Marcus.

"Do you believe that Mr. Rochefort had something to do with Chartwick's non-appearance?"

"I don't know," Artemisia sighed heavily. "All I do know is that when I saw that grin, I…I was so angry that I acted before I thought." But given the opportunity to choose a different course of action, Artemisia was most certain the

only thing she would change was how hard she struck him—
he'd deserved far worse, in her opinion.

"Nigel has spent many hours in this house, and I have
never seen anything to suggest such a vicious nature. The boy
is spoiled, but what good would it serve for him to ruin your
wedding? And besides, you are basing all this on a facial
expression. How do you know it was even directed at you?"

Oh, Artemisia knew! Without a doubt, she *knew*. Ever
since she'd overheard those unkind words spewed from his
mouth all those years ago, she knew. Nigel Rochefort thought
he could poke fun with no consequence to himself. He was
wrong. One day, she *would* prove him wrong.

BACK IN LONDON

Nigel was most certain that Artemisia knew Philippa's
whereabouts. He had to discover what she was hiding. The
gossip was upsetting his mother. He had nothing to do with
Philippa Germayne's mysterious illness, or her removal to the
country, but nonetheless, rumors had flown throughout Town
that he had got her with child and then refused her. All this
trouble because Miss Jerome had seen him in the park with a
crying Philippa. For once in his life, he was innocent of the
scandal being circulated. It just didn't seem fair.

Standing in front of a stark white door, he raised his hand
to the brass knocker. With a firm hand, he brought the handle
down twice in rapid succession. Moments later, a liveried
butler in red opened the door.

"I'm here to see Miss Germayne."

"Wait here. I will see if she is accepting visitors at this
time." Cuthbert showed him the same disdain he had the
previous day.

Nigel watched the butler disappear through a side door. The entrance hall was quite grand, with ceilings that were two stories high, and gilded mirrors which made the large space appear even bigger. However, there was nothing to distinguish it from any other hall in the townhouses of the finest families of the *ton*. For all his time spent in the city, his heart belonged in the country. The estates were more personally decorated… unique.

A monotone voice interrupted his reflections. "This way, Mr. Rochefort. Lord Germayne will see you in his study."

Lord Germayne? No good could possibly come from this meeting. However, it was too late to retreat. Nigel followed the butler down the hall. The black-and-white checkered floor led him farther into the depths of the house, and towards his most certain doom. It was, after all, he who was rumored to be the cause of Philippa's grief. He only hoped Lord Germayne had yet to discover his involvement with the disappearance of Artemisia's fiancé.

The butler halted just outside the study door, allowing Nigel entry. Despite the warm day, a fire had been lit, and the white concoction of fashion about his neck felt suffocating. He went to loosen his cravat and then thought better of it. He did not want to appear nervous or disheveled.

He approached the large mahogany desk, hoping that the other man could not sense his nervousness. "Good afternoon, Lord Germayne."

"Have a seat, Mr. Rochefort." Lord Germayne's voice was firm, in control. This did not bode well. "I understand that you have inquired after Artemisia." Without waiting for Nigel to reply, Lord Germayne continued, "She has left for the country to be with her sister."

Beads of sweat formed on his brow as he stumbled through the words. "And… how does Miss Philippa… what I mean to say is…" Good heavens, he sounded like a bumbling idiot full of guilt.

Lord Germayne's eyes narrowed on him as if delving into the depths of his soul, trying to ascertain what degree of fault was his. Two of his daughters were involved in scandals, and Nigel's name was attached to both. Nigel cleared his throat, preparing to speak, when Lord Germayne shifted some papers across his desk and explained. "You obviously know more than you are trying *not* to let on. Having been acquainted with your family for many years, I know that you would not cause either of my daughters intentional harm, so why don't you just tell me what happened in the park, and why Artemisia struck you in the church."

The first was going to be much easier to explain than the latter. "Three days past, I was riding in the park. I happened across Miss Philippa. She was alone and crying." Nigel saw the concern in Lord Germayne's eyes. He did not know what he could say to ease a father's pain other than to tell him the truth, plain and simple. "She did not say what was upsetting her so. Between sobs, I gathered it was something to do with Artemisia and her wedding. I assumed—" *rather incorrectly it would appear*—"she was upset about her sister's choice of husband, and her own lack of marital prospects. I am no stranger to jealousy. I told her that she was young, and her time would come for marital contentment. I…I also told her to listen to her heart, and to be happy for Artemisia."

"Nothing more?" Lord Germayne's eyes were the most peculiar shade of clear blue. It was most unsettling.

"No, my lord."

Slamming his fist onto the hard surface, Lord Germayne's voice ricocheted off the wood-paneled walls. "Then why is it that every member of the *ton* is talking about how *you* ruined Philippa?"

"I never touched your daughter until that day…. Oh, bloody hell," he cursed, running a frustrated hand through his hair. "What I meant was…" He saw Lord Germayne ease forward in his chair with daggers in his eyes.

Nigel shifted in his seat. This was even more difficult than he'd expected. It brought back unpleasant memories of when he'd been summoned into his father's study as a young boy. He would be made to stand and wait several hours until his father was good and ready to discuss his latest disappointment with his youngest son.

"I offered her advice, a handkerchief, and a brotherly embrace." He paused for a moment, then added with emphasis, "Nothing more."

Lord Germayne sat back in his brown leather chair and eyed him for several moments. "I believe you." His features softened, his words were heartfelt.

Shock and disbelief must have shown on Nigel's face. No one had ever taken him seriously.

"You may be a notorious rake, but your honesty has never been in question. My sister's nephew has nothing but the highest regard for you in that matter," Lord Germayne said.

For a moment, the comment took Nigel aback. He had forgotten that one of his closest friends, and longtime partner in mischief, Marcus, the Marquess of Hawthorne, was connected—albeit only through marriage—to Lord Germayne. Any trouble Nigel had got into over the years had often included Marcus.

Marcus' own father had died when he was just a lad of ten. The late Marquess of Hawthorne had taken him to live with him and his wife at Knollwood. Less than two years later, the marquess had died, leaving Marcus with no male influence to guide him. Lord Germayne had stepped in, offering his assistance to ensure his sister's nephew stayed the course.

"Now that is settled…" Nigel cringed at Lord Germayne's tone that suggested the conversation was about to take a turn for the worse. "Why did Artemisia strike you?"

This was the moment he'd dreaded. What was he to say?

Be honest.

"I believe she suspects that I may have influenced Mr. Chartwick's decision to call off the wedding."

Anger flashed across Lord Germayne's face, followed by a bellow that reached to Nigel's core. "First of all, he did not call off the wedding. The ass *abandoned* her at the altar. Secondly—"

Just then, the very elegant Lady Germayne came dashing into the room. "Albert, you can be heard throughout the house."

This was the second time in so many days that Lady Germayne had inadvertently come to Nigel's rescue.

Coming to a standing position, he bowed and greeted Artemisia's mother. "Good afternoon, Lady Germayne. I do apologize. It appears that I am the source of the ruckus."

"No," she stated with a smile on her face and laughter in her eyes, "I believe my husband is the source."

With a heavy sigh, Lord Germayne stood and walked to where his wife was standing. "I'm sorry, my dear. I'm just worried."

Grief was apparent between the couple. It was evident in their eyes and fatigued postures that neither had slept much since this fiasco began. The dull ache in Nigel's heart that had been plaguing him grew to a pounding thud. He'd caused this. With his selfish interference, he'd caused this, and for what purpose?

For as long as he could remember, he'd argued with

Artemisia. She'd been the thorn in his side. Whenever he'd visited Marcus at Knollwood, she'd been there, interfering with their fun, asking too many questions, and always wanting to tag along.

Once, when she was no more than nine, she had tried to prove she could keep up with Nigel and her cousin. They had dared her to climb a tree, thinking she would not be able to accomplish the feat. But much to Nigel's surprise, not only had she taken the dare, she'd succeeded in scaling the tree. However, returning to the ground was another matter.

Marcus had tried to convince her that the climb down was far simpler, and she just needed to go slowly, but she would not budge. Nigel had glanced up at her, seeing the tears that streamed down her face. She'd begged her cousin to help, but Marcus' idea of helping was to dictate how she should proceed, and to stop crying, which had only served to cause more tears.

Despite Marcus' insistence that Artemisia needed to learn for herself how to get down, Nigel had not been able to watch her suffer any longer. He'd climbed up to where she was, and one branch at a time, guided her downwards. When her feet touched the earth, she was grinning from ear to ear about her accomplishment. On that distant day, their friendship had begun to blossom. That summer holiday had been the fondest of his youth.

What had happened between them? Was he so callous that he thought she did not deserve happiness?

No. She deserved it, and love too, and...

Long buried feelings from the past clawed their way to the surface. There was something else. Something he had desired most of his adult life, but could not admit, not even to himself. It was far easier to play the rake, leaving a trail of mistresses, than to risk his heart.

And then it struck him…

He'd always assumed Artemisia would be there, waiting for him until… His mind wrestled with the thought. She'd always been there for him as a friend, but perhaps there was more to…

"Mr. Rochefort?" The mention of his name brought him out of his musings.

Looking from one grief-stricken parent to the other, Nigel's insides coiled up. This was his fault. The time had come to admit his wrongdoing and set things right.

"Lord Germayne, Lady Germayne, I believe I can rectify this situation."

Lord Germayne opened his mouth, ready to speak, but Lady Germayne interrupted. Pulling on her husband's arm, eyes full of hope, she said, "We would be most grateful for your assistance." She gave her husband a warning look to not interfere before continuing, "Artemisia is at Knollwood."

"Thank you."

And with that farewell, Nigel took his leave, thankful he did not have to explain further. He had been most sincere when he'd stated that he would set things to rights, but he just didn't quite know how to achieve this monumental task, not yet at least. He walked out of the house and into what remained of the day, the smell of horses and fresh roses filling his senses, reminding him of the countryside. Stopping mid-step, something else dawned on him. Lady Germayne had commented that Artemisia was at Knollwood, but there had been no reference to Philippa.

There was something peculiar about Philippa's disappearance, and he intended on getting to the bottom of it—and to put an end to the gossip.

CHAPTER 5

*A*nxious to leave straight away, Nigel wasted no time in returning to Monfort House. Once there, he instructed his valet to pack his things and to meet him at Knollwood. He would travel ahead on horseback with a small satchel.

He was only too glad to leave London. Contrary to what the *ton* believed, he preferred the countryside, the clean air, and peace and quiet. Keeping up his London persona was growing quite tedious. The only reason he had spent so much time in Town was because of his mother, who had not been the same since his father died.

He, himself, had had no love for the man. Truth be told, he'd hated his father. Nothing he ever did was good enough. There had never been kind words, encouragement, or affection of any sort. His only regret was that his father would not be alive to see him prove the old man wrong. And he *would*. He *would* be a kind and thoughtful husband. He *would* be a good father. He would not be a disgrace.

Mile after mile, he brooded about his relationship—or lack thereof—with his father. Although he rode Orazio hard, the horse didn't falter as he galloped. Quite the opposite, in fact. Orazio seemed to have as much pent-up frustration as Nigel. Even so, Nigel would not press his horse to the point of exhaustion. A single night at a coaching inn would suit them both. It would not be wise to arrive at Knollwood and pound on the door in the middle of the night. Lady Hawthorne was a gracious hostess, but kept a strict household, at least where Nigel and Marcus had been concerned.

After a simple meal of roasted pigeon and boiled potatoes, Nigel retired to his room at the Two Swans Inn. Unfortunately, although his body ached and screamed for rest, his mind would not let him relax. Every thought came back to Artemisia.

All his troubles had begun when he'd spoken to Artemisia at Miss Judy Saunders' birthday masque. He had not even wanted to be there, but he'd promised Ranulph, his elder brother, he would keep an eye on Miss Ashurst.

That had been several days before the wedding that was not to be. He hadn't learned yet of Chartwick's change of heart. He tried to recall every word that was spoken during their brief meeting. He remembered seeing Artemisia in the crowded ballroom, looking splendid in cream silk, but her features were distraught. When she'd disappeared through a door behind a large vase, without thought, he'd followed her.

The moment he'd entered the darkened parlor, all he wanted to do was hold her, offer her comfort. But when she'd turned on him and demanded, "Why do you insist on tormenting me?" Nigel's compassion had turned to anger.

He'd blurted out the first thing that came to mind. "Do you love him?"

Why would he care if she loved Chartwick? Love was certainly not a prerequisite in their world.

She'd looked startled at his question. "I like him."

"I will not allow a good friend to marry for 'like.' He deserves more."

"What have I done to earn such hatred? If anything, I should be expressing my hatred for you, Mr. Rochefort."

The words played over and over in his mind. *Hatred.* Why did she dislike him so?

She had tapped her foot with impatience, emphasizing her point. "You have no idea to what I am referring?"

Nigel remembered standing in front of her beautiful form, her auburn hair piled high with delicate curls framing her face. He'd been both baffled *and* confused. "Then what the hell is all this about?"

Even in the dim moonlit parlor, her glare had been evident. But it was when she had turned on her heels, and slammed the door shut with a loud *thud,* leaving him utterly alone that he'd decided she could not marry Chartwick.

He sat up with a start, glancing about the modest inn room. Shadows crept along the walls, clawing at his conscience.

His actions in stopping the wedding had nothing to do with Chartwick claiming he was in love with another. *He'd* decided Artemisia could not marry Chartwick because he deemed her not to be worthy of his friend. But why?

Thinking on it further, his reasons had become numerous —she did not love Chartwick, they would have had a miserable life together, his friend deserved better.

Who could possibly be better than Artemisia?

Nigel tried to shake the confusing thoughts circling in his mind. What was Artemisia to him? She was the niece of Lady Hawthorne, had been a constant annoyance during summer holidays when he escaped his father's disapproving lectures and constant reprimands for Knollwood. She had been like a little sister all those years ago, always underfoot.

But the question remained: why would he want to stop her wedding and ruin her chance at happiness?

Artemisia would not have been happy with Chartwick, that much he was sure of.

She needed to be challenged. Underneath her composed exterior lay an exceptional woman. The problem was, she did not let that person be seen in society. It was only at Knollwood that she seemed her true self.

The last time he had been at Knollwood while Artemisia was in residence was just before her first season. Marcus had invited him to spend Christmastide with him and his aunt, and their extended family. Although Marcus loved his aunt, Nigel suspected the old girl intimidated him. She could be cantankerous, although beneath the outspoken façade lay a heart of gold.

He remembered one evening in particular, as if it were yesterday. When Artemisia had descended the grand staircase, her hand gliding over the polished wood banister, she'd looked like a mischievous sprite in deep green, her lithe form swaying against the soft fabric. Her ample bosom had practically jumped out of the bodice, screaming for attention. It'd taken all his might not to disgrace her, or himself, and give into his desire. That was the first time he saw her, not as a bothersome child, but as a beautiful woman who sent his pulse racing and his heart hammering.

When her nieces had come running up to her, Artemisia's crystal blue eyes had sparkled with delight. He'd been so jealous of the attention she'd given to the children that he'd said some cruel words to her.

"Don't you think that color would suit one of your fair skinned sisters better?" The moment his question had left his mouth, he had regretted it.

The look of hurt that had flashed across her face had

pierced his heart. She had avoided him for the rest of the evening, lavishing all her attention on her little nieces. The only time she had acknowledged him was when her eldest niece, Matilda—who was no more than four at the time, had asked if he would tell her a story about little ponies. Several times during his tale, he'd caught Artemisia looking at him. Her eyes were soft with a longing that he understood all too well.

He'd never meant any of the hurtful words he'd said, but much to his chagrin, he remembered far too many of them. It was only when he'd teased her that she'd paid any attention to him. He realized he was like an insecure schoolboy.

"Bloody hell!" he swore as he jumped out of bed and began pacing the length of the room. It wasn't until this moment that he'd realized how much he craved her attention. How much he craved her. He needed to see her, to atone for past heartaches and mistakes. He prayed that it was not too late.

The night crept on in slow measures. He tried to sleep, but images of Artemisia passed through his mind and stirred a fire within. Her skin was so beautiful. Not the pale, pasty white that was so fashionable amongst the young ladies of the *ton*; hers had a healthy glow. He had often wondered if all of her body looked as if the sun had kissed it. Drifting off to sleep, his last thoughts and images were all of her.

THE NEXT MORNING, Nigel awoke, far from refreshed, to the sound of birds chirping. He had tossed and turned all night. He had not been able to escape thoughts of Artemisia, of all the hurtful words he'd spewed, and his unkind actions over the years. A deep sigh rankled through him. His most recent actions were by far the worst. He was desperate to see her again and correct his past wrongs. Perhaps his mother was right and his feelings for Artemisia had always run far deeper than he was willing to admit. But what *was* his hesitation?

An angry voice from within answered him: *your father*.

Although his parents had appeared to have a loving relationship, his father had not always been kind to Mother. He had *never* been kind to Nigel, treating him like the undeserving spare to a great fortune. All of Lord Monfort's effort and energy had gone into Ranulph. No matter how hard Nigel had tried to make his father notice him, to be proud of him, he'd always failed. Trying to emulate Ranulph had only made matters worse. His father's insults still rang in his ears. *You're nothing like your brother… You're a disgrace to the Rochefort name… Act according to your station.*

As a child, it had not taken Nigel long to discover that he received more attention from his father after stirring trouble. He had often endured an hour-long lecture on proper behavior just to have his father's scrutiny, albeit negative. As a young boy, Nigel had believed if he continued with the mischief, his father would at some point take interest in him. That had never happened.

Years of hurtful words came flooding back. By the time he was a young adult, his father's words had become downright cruel. "You will never amount to anything. You're a scoundrel. No one will ever want you." Only the love given by his mother and brother had seen him through that dark time in his life. Mother had often told him that the reason his father behaved the way he did was because he was jealous of the relationship Nigel had with Ranulph.

"Damn." He cursed out loud.

He was no better than his father. Wasn't that exactly what he had done to Artemisia? As his jealousy and insecurity had risen, he'd attacked her with unkind words. But unlike his father, he *could* change. He would not destroy her life. He would prove to her… and to himself, that he was better than his sire.

By the time he was ready to depart the inn, the sun was high in the sky. If he rode hard again, he would arrive at Knollwood just before dusk. He was hoping to secure an invitation to dine. He wanted more than afternoon tea with Artemisia.

He wanted a lifetime.

With his spirits much lifted, he continued on his way without delay. Even as he enjoyed the gentle summer breeze and peaceful countryside, he could not keep his desire for Artemisia at bay. He was anxious and excited to see her once again. However, after their last meeting, he suspected she would not be pleased to see him again. He had some time before he reached his destination to think of something, some reason for his arrival at Knollwood.

But hours later, with still no plan in place, the impressive estate came into view. The lush green lawns rolled out before him, a path guiding him to his destiny. The vastness of the house beyond was concealed by an elegant façade in varying shades of soft colored brick and dark timber that glowed in the waning sunlight. It was a handsome structure indeed.

He urged Orazio on. The elm tree shaded drive and sloping meadows beyond welcomed the weary traveler. The leaves rustling in the wind were a soothing symphony. Nigel said a silent prayer, hoping that the occupants inside were just as welcoming.

CHAPTER 6

$\mathcal{T}$he afternoon sun had dipped behind a grove of trees, cooling the Green Parlor. A fire had been lit, but its effects had yet to be felt. Artemisia reclined on her favorite pink damask chaise. It had been a wonderful day spent in her aunt's company. They had walked about the grounds, picnicked under the large oak tree in the center courtyard, and picked roses. But despite how relaxed her body felt, her mind was full of thoughts, dark and foreboding, as if something troublesome was looming on the horizon.

A long, deep breath exited her aunt's mouth. Artemisia sat up quickly, startled by the sound. "Is anything the matter? Would you like a cushion?"

"My dear, perhaps you have not taken notice, but the good Lord has already provided me with plenty of 'cushion'."

Artemisia heard her own laughter ring through the room. It had been a long time—too long—since she'd laughed like this. Relaxing back, she sighed. Knollwood was good for what ailed her.

Simms, the head butler, walked into the room holding an elegant scalloped-edged silver tray. Stopping in front of Aunt

Lou, he lowered the tray, revealing a folded sheet of paper. Artemisia watched her aunt take the note and read it, before responding with excitement, "Show him in Simms." Aunt Lou did not clarify who had just arrived, leaving Artemisia to wonder.

Minutes later, the 'who' in question strolled into the room. Artemisia's heart quickened when Nigel Rochefort, the very bane of her existence, sauntered in, looking relaxed and far too handsome by half.

"Good afternoon, Lady Hawthorne." The enthusiasm in his voice and bright smile were almost too much to bear. His deep blue eyes twinkled with mischief as he turned his attention to Artemisia. "Good afternoon, Miss Germayne."

A fluttering in her stomach, followed by sweaty palms and a dry throat, assaulted her being. She was not prepared to see *him*. She was only beginning to come to terms with what had happened in London. Nigel Rochefort was a most unwelcome guest, in her opinion.

Obviously, her aunt thought otherwise. "Dear boy, it has been far too long."

"My sentiments exactly." His flashing smile might charm Aunt Lou, but Artemisia would not be fooled.

"If you were hoping to see Marcus, he won't be arriving until two days hence." It was a dismissive remark, but Artemisia did not care. She would not make this visit pleasant for him, especially not after all he had done.

She watched Nigel fumble through his words. "I… Oh, yes. I…I was hoping to meet up with him. Our letters must have crossed. I thought we were to rendezvous here before… before going to Bath." He looked everywhere but at Artemisia or Aunt Lou. He was a horrid liar. It was quite obvious that he had some other intention. With any hope, her aunt would see through his façade and send him on his way.

"Please join us for tea."

Or not.

Giving Artemisia a sideways glance, he took the seat across from her. "That is most generous."

The afternoon only continued to deteriorate. Artemisia listened with half an ear as her aunt and Nigel conversed about the pleasant weather, the anticipation of a good harvest, and the building of a new stable at Nigel's estate, Kettleworth.

What is he doing here? She did not believe for one moment he'd arranged to meet Marcus at Knollwood. Her aunt's nephew had sent word only this afternoon that his plans had changed, and he would be arriving in two days' time.

Perhaps the gossip in Town was too much for him, and he had to escape. Or better yet, perhaps he'd been run out of Town. That would serve him right, meddling in her family's affairs.

Artemisia was so caught up in the image of Nigel being chased by women with clubs and men with swords that she did not hear the remainder of the conversation.

"Artemisia… Artemisia," her aunt called to her. Aunt Lou leaned closer, but was still several feet away, when she murmured under her breath, "Why don't you invite Mr. Rochefort to dine with us?"

Artemisia glanced up and saw Nigel staring at them. She was most certain that he'd heard her aunt's request. She detested being put on the spot like this. What was she supposed to say? She knew what she would like to say: *I would rather dine with a pig than spend the evening in Mr. Rochefort's company.* But that wouldn't do. She settled for politeness. "Mr. Rochefort, won't you please stay for dinner?"

"That is most kind, but I must decline at this time. I have yet to secure accommodation…."

Her sigh of relief was cut short when her aunt stopped him mid-sentence and exclaimed, "Pshaw! You must stay at Knollwood. I am sure Arte will not mind, and Marcus will be arriving within a matter of days. It will be just like old times."

Artemisia would have liked to disagree with her aunt, but good manners had been drilled into her. Aunt Lou and Nigel looked at her in anticipation of a response. Again, she settled for something other than the truth. "That would be most… pleasant."

Reaching for the silver bell on the side table, Aunt Lou started, "Dinner is at eight in the newly renovated Yellow Dining Room." The bell sent out a sharp, high-pitched sound. When Simms appeared in the doorway, she gave instructions. "See Mr. Rochefort to the Orange Chamber."

Artemisia watched Nigel follow Simms out of the room and waited a couple of minutes before she questioned her aunt. "Why did you ask him to stay?"

"He has stayed often enough over the years. Besides, I thought you might enjoy the company of someone closer to your own age."

Nigel was the last person in the world that she wanted to spend any time with. And to make matters worse, he was ensconced in a bedchamber in the family wing, directly across the hall from her room. A gripping tightness constricted her insides. She could hardly breathe. What was her aunt thinking?

AT TEN MINUTES OF EIGHT, Nigel was still wandering through the halls, looking for the Yellow Dining Room, when he spotted Artemisia exiting the Green Parlor. She wore a simple gown of pale yellow that accentuated her olive skin. Long auburn tendrils caressed her neck. She was breathtaking.

"May I escort you to dinner?" Nigel extended his arm, waiting for her to accept.

"Why are you here?" Her tone matched her eyes, uncaring and harsh. It was not the manner he had hoped for, but more like the one he knew he deserved.

"I've come to make amends."

She eyed him with contempt. "I don't want apologies. I just want *you* to leave me alone."

"That is the furthest thing from my mind." It was a bold statement, but he wanted to make his intentions at least somewhat known.

Artemisia started to slide away from him, but Nigel grabbed her arm and pulled her into his embrace. He held her there, felt her breathing increase against his chest. She was close, close enough to kiss. He felt a subtle stirring deep in his groin. *Damn.* He had to refrain. Well, at least for the time being.

He took in a slow breath to steady his thoughts, then leaned in and whispered into her ear, "Truce."

She gave him a wary look. The distrust in her eyes unsettled his nerves.

"I did not come here to cause you grief." He waited for some response or retort. When none came, he added, "Can we at least pretend to be civil for your aunt's sake?"

Her features softened. He'd known that she would not want to do anything that would upset her aunt. Releasing her, but still blocking her passage, he offered his arm once again, giving her little opportunity to reject him.

She took his arm with caution. "Truce."

She was like a skittish puppy, and he was going to have to

earn her trust. The problem was, he didn't quite know where to begin. Confess all his past sins? No, that would only serve to push her away. He wanted to win her over, show her that he had changed and was not the rake the world thought him to be.

He led her down the hall, glancing into each room they passed. Unfortunately, none were lit. *Where the bloody hell was the dining room?*

"You don't know where the Yellow Dining Room is, do you?"

Laughing at her frankness, he confessed, "I've been roaming these halls for almost half an hour and have yet to discover where the elusive, newly renovated, Yellow Dining Room might be."

Artemisia joined in his laughter. It was not the delicate, prissy laugh that all the young ladies of the *ton* affected, and that he detested. It was rich and hearty and came from deep within.

"And what do you find so amusing?"

"You obviously have forgotten my aunt's quirks. You could roam this house for days and never find a dining room with a décor that is yellow."

"You're right, I did forget." When he laughed again, he felt her fingers stroke across his sleeve. Desire shot through him. Stamping down the urge to pull her back into his embrace and kiss her senseless, he tried to focus on the conversation. "So, what color *is* the Yellow Dining Room?"

When she glanced up at him, he was struck by how alike her crystal blue eyes were to her father's. He had never noticed the similarity before. But where Lord Germayne's gaze was unsettling, set against her enticing olive skin, Artemisia's was seductive and mystical.

She must have sensed the direction in which his mind was

traveling. In the next moment, she tried to withdraw her hand, but he placed his on top of it. Caressing with a gentle stroke, he leaned in and murmured into her ear, "Truce, remember?"

When she finally answered his question, her response was short and curt. "Blue."

The struggle within was apparent. He stood on unsteady ground. He did not want her to be angry—or rather, angrier—with him. He had to do something to ease the tension simmering between them, so he decided to try his hand at humor. "But of course, that makes perfect sense. Yellow and blue are often mistaken for being the same, especially when discussing a cloudless day." He was rewarded with her sweet laughter.

He was making progress.

DINNER in the Yellow Dining Room, decorated in blue, with not even a speck of yellow to be seen, was a most formal affair. A large brick and wood fireplace stood as sentinel at the center of one wall, while elaborate candelabras illuminated the space, adding warmth and comfort. Ornate cupboards in rich mahogany graced the perimeter, and fine bone china embellished in a blue floral pattern was displayed with pride on the obliging sideboard. Fresh cut roses from Artemisia's earlier outing graced the center of the long rectangular dining table, and the candlelight flickered across its highly polished surface like stars in the night. It was all too perfect.

In such a serene environment, Artemisia should have been at ease, but that was not the case this evening. Even the width of the dining table and dim light could not hide the anxiety quivering inside of her. Why did he keep looking at her? And when he'd whispered that single word into her ear only a short time ago, she'd been certain that she'd felt his breath invade a deep, forgotten place in her soul.

Throughout the first course, she attempted to avoid eye contact with him, but she could not shake the feeling that he was staring at her. Common sense gave way to curiosity. She glanced up from the *Ragout à la Français* on her plate and met his eyes.

His gaze was intense and filled with an emotion unfamiliar to her. She had complete faith in Maggie's abilities to dress her so that she looked presentable, but she could not help but wonder if something was missing from her attire. The way he kept surveying her from across the table was most unsettling.

Aunt Lou appeared to take no notice. "So, dear boy, tell me all the news of your family. How is your mother?"

"Better, thank you." His voice was laced with love and affection, two emotions that Artemisia had been most certain he did not possess. "The death of my father has taken its toll, but with my brother now engaged to Miss Ashurst, she has found new life in helping to plan the wedding."

"Ah, that's right. Poor dear's mother passed away quite some time ago." Aunt Lou took a mouthful of ragout. "Well, I am glad for her. Sweet girl... sweet girl."

Artemisia paid no attention to the conversation. Nigel's presence at Knollwood had disrupted her senses more than usual, and she was trying to work out why. She was convinced that he had something to do with her fiancé's abandonment. But, if he *were* somehow responsible, why would he come to Knollwood? He must have known she would be here. Her heart leapt with excitement. Could he have come just for her?

No, most certainly not, she reminded herself. Had he not mentioned earlier that he planned to meet Marcus here? *Oh bother!* She did not know what to think, especially with the way he had been eyeing her all night. Part of her desperately wanted to believe that he had come to see *her*, that he truly wanted to make amends for past hurts.

When at last she and her aunt adjourned to the Green Parlor, her head was throbbing from all the unanswered questions and emotions coursing through her. She wanted to be angry with Nigel, but something deeper, something she could not even begin to explain, called forth a different emotion. Something she dared not to hope for.

CHAPTER 7

*T*he next morning Artemisia emerged from her room, far from refreshed, having tossed and turned most of the night. She had not felt this restless since the beginning of her first season, when her prospects had seemed so bright.

With gentle footsteps, she made her way to the library. She did not want to encounter her aunt or Nigel. She wanted solitude. Opening the door with ease, she snuck into the cool space and closed the door behind her. Light from the partially opened curtains provided a path to the French doors. This was one of her favorite rooms at Knollwood; the smell of books was like being with a trusted friend.

Reaching for the curtains, she felt the thickness of their weight between her fingers and pulled them wide, the warmth from the sun cascading across her face. Opening the door, she emerged onto a secluded terrace. The surrounding country-side was so peaceful, the perfect balm to soothe her rumpled soul.

That peace, however, did not last for long.

She turned around at the sound of footsteps emerging onto the terrace.

Nigel.

"What are you doing here?" She had yet to recover from her ill-spent night, and the last thing she wanted to do was entertain an unwanted guest.

"Your aunt told me where to find you."

"That's not what I meant." She had to know why he was here. Regardless of the answer, she had to know. "Why did you come to Knollwood?"

He stepped in closer to her. "I told you, I want to make amends for what I have done."

Would he confess? Narrowing her gaze, she asked in an accusatory tone, "And what have you done?"

"Ruined your sister…"

"That's only a rumor."

"Where is she then? Your parents mentioned she was here with you."

"Umm…" How had he turned the situation against her? She wanted answers from *him*, not the other way around. She would give him his answers, and then demand that he leave Knollwood. "She is visiting a friend." It wasn't a lie. Philippa and Mr. Keates *were* friends.

"Friends… I see. Well, I guess I will have to wait for her to return to apologize for my behavior and clear my good name."

She could hardly contain her laughter. "Your good name? Your name is synonymous with scandal!"

"Perhaps I have a new outlook on life." As he took another step closer, her heart started to pound in her chest. "Perhaps I want more than to be known as a scoundrel. Making amends to your sister for the trouble I have caused is the first step."

The look in his eyes made her chest tighten. She was guilty of keeping Philippa's actions a secret. He seemed sincere, but her heart reminded her that he could not be trusted. "It could be a while."

"I have all the time in the world." He took another step towards her, his eyes darkening with a look unfamiliar to her. Now, they were a mere couple of feet away from each other. "I didn't come just to apologize to Philippa."

"Oh?" Her breaths came in short little spurts. "Why… why else did you come?"

"Because of—"

"Excuse me, Miss Germayne," the parlor maid's voice sounded from inside the library, "Lady Hawthorne is inquiring after you."

Without so much as a single word, Artemisia turned on her heel and walked away. Part of her had wanted to stay and discover what Nigel was about to say, but then again, she was in no mood for any of his games. She truly could not risk her heart, not again. It would be for the best *if* she remembered that. *If.*

She found her aunt in the Green Parlor, entrenched beneath a mountain of cloth and embroidery. "You wanted to see me?"

"Oh, there you are, Arte. Mrs. Bing was delivered of her baby three weeks early." Aunt Lou waved her hand at the disarray of material surrounding her before continuing, "All these were supposed to be completed before the joyous arrival. Would you mind…?"

Not waiting for her aunt to finish her sentence, she took a seat and got straight to work.

She was enjoying what remained of the morning, when Aunt Lou asked, "Do you think it will be long before we hear how *she* is fairing?"

The 'she' in Aunt Lou's question, Artemisia inferred to mean, was Philippa. Although Aunt Lou preferred not to know every detail—so that when her brother questioned her, she could answer with honesty—she did have some knowledge of Philippa's scheme.

"I suspect she will send word once all is settled. I only hope Father will not be too displeased with her actions."

Shrugging her shoulders, Aunt Lou replied, "She is the youngest, and the youngest always gets away with more."

Artemisia was all too familiar with that mentality. Eyeing her aunt, she was about to comment about her father being the youngest of their siblings, but before she could begin her teasing, Nigel walked in.

"Who is the youngest?" he questioned with suspicion.

Artemisia hoped her face gave nothing away, but she was surprised by his arrival in her aunt's parlor. She was about to tell him another lie, but something inside stopped her. Instead, she skirted the question. "Oh, we were just discussing the adventurous nature of younger siblings."

Nigel gave her a peculiar look. She wondered if he suspected they had been discussing Philippa.

She fumbled through an explanation that she hoped made some sort of sense. "Both my sisters have had their fair share of adventures, but I am the middle sister, the sensible one. I keep my feet firmly on the ground and…"

Nigel eyed her skeptically. He sat down on the settee, inspecting his hand with great interest before asking, "I was just wondering if you have heard from your younger, adventurous sister?"

"No… why… I mean, she's visiting a friend and…" She swallowed hard. "Why?"

His eyes met hers. "I am most anxious to clear my name." With that final statement, he stood and walked away.

Her aunt eyed her with suspicion and Artemisia realized if she was not careful, she might end up wanted for a crime she did not commit. "Would you care to tell me what all that was about?"

"No."

"No?" Her aunt raised a brow in question.

Sidestepping the real issue, Artemisia waved her hand in a nonchalant manner. "Oh, he was just inquiring after Philippa." She did not know why she could not be honest and just tell her aunt the whole story. If there was anyone she could trust, it was Lou. But confiding in her would only raise more questions. Questions she did not have answers to. Everything in her world had been turned upside down over the past few days. Inwardly shaking her head, she decided silence was better.

THEY HAD AVOIDED each other for the better part of the day, but the dinner hour was approaching, and Artemisia would have to face Nigel. The moment he entered the room, her heart slammed in her chest and her hands trembled. She did not know how she would survive the evening.

She tried to keep her attention focused on her food, but Nigel's constant gaze unsettled her. By the time they had finished the dessert of sugared apples, she thought she would melt under the heat of his stare. Why was he acting thusly?

Without warning, Aunt Lou backed her chair away from the table, over the expensive rug, and stood. Nigel, in turn, stood and glanced about in confusion.

"I'm feeling rather spent." Her aunt looked from Artemisia to Nigel with a mischievous gleam in her eye.

Artemisia could not help but wonder if Aunt Lou had an ulterior motive.

"If you will excuse me, I will retire for the evening." The older lady started towards the door, then turned around and addressed them both, "Enjoy the rest of the evening."

And with that, Artemisia found herself alone with Nigel Rochefort, rake extraordinaire.

NIGEL WAS STILL STANDING, completely astonished. He could not believe his good fortune that Lady Hawthorne had decided to retire for the evening, leaving him alone with Artemisia. However, before he even had the chance to enjoy the serendipity, Artemisia stood, her napkin still in hand. Her eyes darted about the room, as if looking for a reason to escape.

"I'm rather tired myself. I believe…"

Hastily, he rushed to her side. Placing a firm hand on her bare shoulder, he pleaded, "Please don't go."

Her clear blue eyes looked at him in question, and then turned downward toward where skin met skin. His hand burned with the need to explore. Without thought or regard for the consequence, he leaned his head in and brushed a light kiss across her lips. She tasted like sweet apples with a hint of cinnamon.

Artemisia stumbled back, the shock and surprise clear on her face. Without saying a word, she fled from the room.

"Damn," he swore, shoving the chair into its place.

CLUTCHING the napkin to her pounding chest, Artemisia ran from the dining room. She could not believe what had just occurred. He'd kissed her. What had he been thinking? She was not some loose tart he could have his way with. It was just a game to him. Other's emotions always had been. He cared naught for who he hurt or the rumors that followed. He only cared about his next conquest. Well, she would not fall victim to that.

She'd had enough gossip to last a lifetime. All that she desired was the quiet country life. Besides, she still had her sister to think about. When the *ton* discovered what Philippa had done, she suspected the tittle-tattle would force her entire family to retire to the country.

When she reached the family wing, she decided to call in on her aunt before retiring for the evening. She suspected Aunt Lou's performance at dinner was just a ploy. She did not want her relative to have any misconceptions about herself and Nigel.

Approaching her aunt's suite, she could see candlelight streaming from under the door. After a gentle knock, she asked, "May I come in?"

Pushing the door wide, she saw her aunt sitting by the fire, working on her embroidery. Beautiful shades of purple encompassed the room. She walked across the well-cushioned rug and stood before Lou.

"Are you well this evening? It is not like you to retire early."

"I am fine, dear girl." Her aunt changed the subject. "I couldn't help but notice what a handsome gentleman Nigel has turned out to be."

Ah, so there was an ulterior motive. "I never really thought much about him." That was *the* lie of lies. Artemisia had thought of Nigel often over the years, far too often. What girl wouldn't? One would have to be blind not to notice his handsome face, blond hair, and deep blue eyes. He was fashioned like a god from mythology. He was *also* arrogant, selfish, and an absolute rake. His reputation with the ladies was notorious. If the most handsome debutantes of the *ton* had yet to hold his interest, there was no hope for her.

But he *had* just kissed her only moments ago. Although it was a game, nothing more, she reminded herself. She would not succumb to his cruel intentions.

Taking extreme interest in the handkerchief she was working upon, Aunt Lou did not venture to look up before she began to speak. "I believe I will visit Mrs. Hart tomorrow. Her husband passed away two months ago, and she has been so distraught. You are welcome to join me, but I think you might find a more pleasant diversion here."

Was her aunt trying to play matchmaker now? Artemisia did not want to argue. Besides, an argument with her aunt always ended with herself on the losing side. "I am sure I can find some way to occupy my day." Aunt Lou's head snapped up in utter surprise. She must have assumed that Artemisia would put up more of an argument. No, she would not give her aunt the satisfaction. Instead, she would just humor her relative. It was the easiest way out of her current predicament. "The rose garden *is* in dire need of attention."

She hid her grin as annoyance flashed across her aunt's face. "If that's how you want to waste the day away, it is not my place to interfere."

Bending down, she kissed her beloved aunt on the cheek. "Good night, Aunt Lou."

CHAPTER 8

*M*aggie came rushing into Artemisia's room at the appalling hour of half after six in the morning. "This just arrived," she squealed, her voice far too chipper for this uncivilized time.

Still groggy from sleep, Artemisia took the missive. Rubbing her eyes with one hand, she stared at the letter. Recognizing her sister's handwriting, her stomach churned, and anxiety edged its way up her throat. All this secretiveness was going to be her undoing. With unsteady hands, she broke the seal.

My dearest Arte,
All is progressing as planned.
With all my love,
P.K.

All Artemisia's own heartache was worth it just to know her sister was about to be married to the man she loved. She lay back on the feather pillows. So much had changed in the last weeks. When Philippa had come to her, desperate to find a way to marry Mr. Keates, she had not fathomed the turn of events occurring in her own life. Reaching out, she picked up a brush from the nightstand and began to run it through her hair, the words from her favorite Italian love song flowing from her mouth.

Everything would turn out for the best.

SEVERAL HOURS PASSED before Artemisia emerged from her room. She had dilly-dallied the morning away with the hope of avoiding Nigel. She was still flustered and confused by his kiss last evening. By the time she ventured into the breakfast room, she was informed that her aunt had already broken her fast and left for the day.

Bearing a scone and jam from the sideboard, she was about to take a seat at the table when she heard a familiar whistle coming from the hall. She just knew it was Nigel, come to torture her. Wrapping her scone in a napkin, she slipped into the servants' hall that connected the breakfast room to the kitchen, and scurried down the passage towards the smell of fresh-baked bread. When she reached the kitchen, she felt certain that Nigel would not have known of her presence in the breakfast room.

The problem was how would she avoid seeing him during the entire day. There was only one place she could hide—the Oak Courtyard.

Knollwood had been designed around three courtyards— the center one being the most important and the heart of the house. It had never been opened to guests or visitors, having always been reserved for the exclusive use of the family. Only they and trusted servants knew the whereabouts of the secret door that led to its private enclosure.

Winding her way through the depths of the house, she looked over her shoulder at every turn. When at last she reached the Great Hall, she paused, and glanced both ways. She wanted to insure no one—or to be more precise, Nigel—had followed. Slipping behind the large tapestry that told the tale of the Great Oak, she felt for the handle, pushed the door slightly open before slipping into the dark passageway. Before too long, she reached the end, and coaxed the exterior door open with gentle ease, emerging onto the large, sunlit center courtyard.

Its perimeter was a veritable sea of red, pink, and white roses. Generation after generation of marchionesses had planted rose bushes. Their sweet scent intoxicated the air, while busy bees went about their work.

In the middle of the courtyard stood a single oak tree, hundreds of years old. A heart had been etched into the bark generations before with the initials 'N & A'. Artemisia had always loved this tree. Having one of the same initials, she'd often dreamed it was an omen of whom she might marry. Once, many years ago, she'd fancied the 'N' stood for Nigel. That was, until his hurtful words had cracked the lining of her heart.

When Artemisia was a young girl, she'd often begged Aunt Lou to tell her the story of the Great Oak. Legend had it that Knollwood had been designed around the tree. The first Lady Hawthorne—brought here as a bride—was so distraught when her husband went to war, she watered the Great Oak with her tears, praying daily for his safe return. Many years passed and still she did not know if her husband had lived or died. But no-one else could tempt her steadfast heart. When at last Lord Hawthorne returned home unharmed, a great celebration took place. But on the night of the festivities, a terrible thunderstorm shook the land, and lightning lit up the sky. When dawn approached, it was seen that Lord and Lady Hawthorne's initials were burned into the bark of the tree by the lightning—a sign from the heavens above that the two lovers would live a long and prosperous life together.

Artemisia had always doubted that lightning could be so creative, but she loved the story, nonetheless. Through the generations, other lovers had carved their initials onto the trunk, with the hope that they too would be blessed with a happy union.

Approaching the tree, Artemisia stood on an obliging exposed root. Reaching out with her finger, she traced the heart and initials. Would she ever find a love like theirs? Would anyone ever love her for who she was, how she looked? She sat down on the root, pulled the scone from the napkin, and ate her breakfast. When she was finished, she reread her sister's note. In spite of everything, she was happy for Philippa. A deep sigh coursed through her body. She only wished she could find her own happiness. Resting her head against the rough bark, she closed her eyes, lost in the sweet scent of roses and dreaming of her own love.

NIGEL EMERGED into the courtyard and spotted Artemisia. She was a vision from another time and place. She sat on an exposed root, her head resting against the tree. Her hair was fastened with a pale pink ribbon at the base of her neck. How he would love to untie that ribbon and run his fingers through her auburn locks.

The sun filtered through the branches, resting on her. For the first time, he noticed that her hair was not only deep auburn, but streaked with highlights of gold. Her skin was the most enticing shade of olive. Her voluptuous body was made for the pleasures he could show her. He shook his head, trying to stamp down the lust and regain his composure. He'd already scared her off once; he did not want her to run away as she had done last night.

Approaching with caution, trying not to alarm her, he strolled up to where she sat. He took another step, watching her chest rise and fall with each peaceful breath.

A twig snapped underfoot.

Her head shot up. Confused blue eyes met his.

She crossed her arms and snapped at him. "What are you doing here?" He saw her fumble with a piece of paper, shoving it beneath the folds of her pink dress.

"Your aunt told me that you often spent part of your day here. She thought you might enjoy my company." He hadn't even asked for Lady Hawthorne's help or advice on winning her niece. When they'd come across each other this morning in the breakfast room, Lady Hawthorne had volunteered Artemisia's usual itinerary. He did not know why Lady Hawthorne wanted to help, but appreciated the unsolicited assistance, nonetheless.

"This is a private garden, for the exclusive use of the family." She narrowed her gaze. "What is it that you want?"

"Your aunt gave me permission to join you." She appeared uneasy at that remark. Perhaps it had something to do with that note. What was she hiding? "Is it so hard to believe that I want to be in your company?"

Skepticism filled her clear blue eyes. He wasn't about to back down. How would he ever win her affections if he let her dictate where and when they could see each other?

Her gaze softened a moment before she resigned herself to his company. "I suppose not."

Waving his hand in the direction of the vacant space beside her, he asked with a combination of hope and hesitation, "May I?"

Her acceptance came not in words, but with a slightly unsure nod of her head.

"Your aunt mentioned something about a legend connected with this tree. Would you mind telling it?"

Nigel knew that she did mind. If this had been her house and she had her way, he was most certain that she would have tossed him out on his arse the moment he'd arrived. But proper manners won, and with some reluctance, she told him of the story of the oak tree.

When it ended, he stood and reached out his hand to hers. She stared at his outstretched fingers as if they were snakes.

"It won't bite, it is just my hand. I thought you might enjoy a walk. It is a fine day." He gave her one of his notorious rakish smiles in the hope that would soften her resolve towards him.

When she placed her petite, ungloved hand in his, it was as if a bolt of lightning careened through his body. And even better, she did not pull her fingers from his. It was a positive beginning. Now he just had to control the searing urge to kiss her. But matters were only made worse when she stood and brushed the backside of her dress. *Oh, dear Lord.* He imagined what it would be like to run his hand over her smooth naked flesh, what she would taste—

"Are you quite alright, Mr. Rochefort?"

He cleared his throat. "Yes." Offering his arm, he asked, "Shall we?" He led her back toward the secret doorway while making casual conversation. He was trying to be a perfect gentleman despite the flurry of desire that ran rampant through his mind. "Lady Hawthorne suggested a walk by the lake. Is that destination acceptable?"

"That would be most pleasant, Mr. Rochefort." Her manners were impeccable and formal, much to his chagrin. He wanted her to relax, to open up to him, to trust him.

"Why must we be so formal? Our families have a long-standing friendship. Have we not known each other since we were children? Did I not rescue you from the clutches of an overbearing tree in your youth?"

Artemisia teased, her voice light and airy. "I had not realized that I was in such dire circumstances all those years ago."

He puffed out his chest and in a valiant voice replied, "A lady in distress is always a dire circumstance."

"I'm sure you have had your fair share of ladies in distress over the years." Her voice was full of hurt.

Nigel brought her to a halt and turned her to face him. "I don't want to argue. I don't want to relive some unfortunate episode from the past. I just want to spend the day enjoying your company. No pretense, no formalities, or social constrictions. Just two friends. I believe a truce was declared, after all."

The thought of being 'just' friends was odd. Nigel had never had any female friends, never trusted any woman to want to only be friends without it leading to marriage. But with Artemisia, he wanted friendship. No, not only friendship, more than friendship. He wanted to know what she liked, what made her laugh, her hopes and dreams. He wanted intimacy and… He just wanted Artemisia.

THE DAY PROVED to be rather warm. They took their time walking through the rose garden. Nigel had a vast knowledge of flowers, courtesy of his mother, Artemisia was informed. She enjoyed this side of him—it was like old times.

By the time they reached the lake, little beads of sweat were forming on her brow. She knew she must look frightful. Nigel, however, looked splendid. Not a blond blade of hair was out of place, and no signs of weariness marked his features. He had always surrounded himself with the most beautiful of women—albeit opera singers, mistresses, and widows who cared naught for their reputations, but they were exquisite just the same. Artemisia could not hold a candle to those ladies.

"There is a gazebo on the other side. Would you care to sit awhile?"

She must look worse than she thought if he was suggesting a rest. Self-conscious about her disheveled appearance, she responded in a hushed tone, "Yes." Although she did not wish to look at herself in a mirror, she would have liked a moment to set herself to rights.

The gazebo sat atop a slight slope that led down to the lake. Her aunt had always enjoyed sitting out here, closer to nature, and ordered that the structure be in good order for her daily pleasure.

Walking around the perimeter of the lake was most enjoyable. A cool breeze skimmed over the water, easing some of Artemisia's discomfort. When they reached the slope where the gazebo sat, they began to walk up the slight incline. Nigel released her hand and turned around.

"Isn't it breath—?"

Artemisia did not hear the rest of his sentence. One moment she was standing, feeling a bit lightheaded, and the next she'd lost her footing and was tumbling backwards, right into the lake.

Before she even realized what had happened, strong arms lifted her from the water. "Are you alright?" His voice was full of concern, and his eyes held an unfamiliar but enticing look.

Her breathing became heavier when his fingers brushed the side of her breast. *Oh dear!* That brief touch sent a ripple of tingles all the way down to her very wet toes. "Yes, I think so. I… I lost my footing."

Nigel carried her away from the water's edge and placed her with gentle ease on the grass. Her gown was ruined, her ego bruised. She was an utter disaster. What must he think of her?

He sat down beside her. "That was rather refreshing, don't you think?" His voice was filled with a hint of humor.

He wasn't teasing or poking fun at her. This was the Nigel she knew from years ago—kind and charismatic. "Yes, quite so," she said with a giggle.

"Shall we abandon the gazebo and walk back to the house?"

"Perhaps avoiding the lake altogether," she suggested.

Nigel stood, and with a gallant voice, declared, "Anything my lady desires."

Taking her hands in his, he helped her into a standing position. Her heart beat in a rapid staccato that even the busy bees would be jealous of. They stood there for what felt like an eternity. Artemisia did not want the moment to end. Warmth and excitement began to bubble from within as his hands caressed her. She had never felt this way before. It both frightened and excited her.

A moment later, the spell was broken when a pair of king-fishers shrilled overhead. He bent down to retrieve something that must have fallen out of his pocket, and then offered his arm to her.

Artemisia was thankful for the silent walk back to the house. She wanted nothing more than the quiet of her room and to strip off her wet gown and take a hot bath to contemplate all these foreign emotions surging through her body.

WHEN NIGEL ENTERED HIS ROOM, he took the wet scrap of paper from his jacket and placed it on the small writing desk by the window. Smoothing out the note, he tried to make out the words. He wondered what information had captivated Artemisia so much. She'd looked so beautiful when he'd first spied her with her eyes closed, head resting against the oak tree. He wanted her daydreams to be of him.

Most of the ink had smeared. Only two words were recognizable—*my love.*

My love?

Jealousy burned through his body. She could not possibly have a new love. She had been intended for Chartwick. Could she have a secret lover? A vein in his neck pulsed with each breath. Who was this *love*?

Perhaps Lady Hawthorne could shed some light on the subject. He was not going to let anyone stand in his way to win her heart. Anxious energy settled in his chest, and he paced the length of the room several times before determining his next course of action. Despite any obstacles, including the lady herself, Artemisia would be his.

CHAPTER 9

*T*he next day, Lady Hawthorne left a note saying she had been called away to visit another friend. Nigel thought it peculiar that she was spending so much time away from Knollwood, but was thankful for the time alone with Artemisia. The Great Oak had become his favorite spot to enjoy her company.

Once again, her head rested against the trunk of the tree, and her were eyes closed as if in deep contemplation. Without opening her eyes, she questioned in a very small quiet voice, "Why do you think I was not good enough for Chartwick?"

Guilt tightened and constricted his around his heart. Nigel felt as if he would be damned for all eternity. He was responsible for her current heartache. "Who said you were not good enough?"

Her eyes shot open and pierced his. He sucked in his breath, trying to squash his guilt. His actions had caused her grief. Would she forgive him when she discovered the truth?

"He abandoned me on our wedding day. What else am I to think?"

"That he is an idiot." His simple statement made her

giggle. "You have dimples." He did not mean to say it aloud, but he had never noticed them before. Perhaps it was because she was either shouting at him or hiding behind a composed façade. He should have remembered them. He made her laugh often enough when they were children. *You weren't in love with her then.*

"I'm sorry." Her apology came out as a mere whisper.

Why was she embarrassed, he wondered? Because of the dimples? His thoughts wandered as he watched her. The blush across her cheeks was most alluring. Reaching out, he caressed her cheek. "Don't be." Artemisia's body relaxed, and her lips parted. He felt the heat growing between the two of them. He wanted to kiss her. But before he could act upon his urge, she turned away.

He took in a heavy breath. He did not want her to turn away. He wanted her to confide in him, share her hopes and dreams, but she seemed so unsure of herself… of him.

Worrying the edge of her dress, she asked with hesitation, "Do you think he did not want to marry me because I am such a horrid dancer?"

"That is the most ridiculous…" She glared at him, daring him to lie to her. "Alright, so you are not the most graceful dancer."

"That is the mildest way I have ever heard anyone describe my lack of coordination." Although she was smiling, he could see the anguish in her eyes.

Standing up, he grabbed her hands and pulled her up, stepping toward her so they were standing face to face.

"What are you doing?" The deep blush on her face high-lighted the shock in her voice.

"I am going to teach you to dance." His mother had once told him the way to a woman's heart was through dancing. If that were true, then Nigel could think of no better way to reach Artemisia's.

Trying to pull away from him, she protested, "There is no music."

He would not take no for an answer. "Shall I hum a tune?"

Her laughter rang through the courtyard.

"I will take your laughter as meaning no."

He began to pull her towards flatter ground when she pleaded, "I don't want to… Please, let me…"

"Why not?"

She looked around as if searching for some reason to decline his offer. Her eyes widened. "It would not be proper."

"That is just an excuse." He stood there eyeing her, waiting for her to reveal her hesitation. He knew if he stared at her long enough, her resolve would weaken. And sure enough, it did.

Looking down at the ground, her words were faint. "It won't help. I have had dozens of dancing lessons." She turned her head away, avoiding eye contact. Looking across the courtyard, she confessed, "Each lesson ended the same way—wrong steps, crushed toes, and mocking laughter."

Nigel cupped her cheek and turned her head toward him. "It will be different this time." He guided her away from the tree's exposed roots as she tried to pull her hand from his.

"I will not take 'no' for an answer." Despite her unwillingness, he began the lesson. "We will start with a simple *Chassé Step*." He explained the movements to her, showed her what to do, and then watched her try to mimic the steps on her own.

"Good. Next is the *Jeté Assemblé*." Again, he repeated the same exercise, but she faltered through the movements.

He took her hands to give her more stability as she tried

to leap from her front foot while moving her back foot forward into third position.

The space between her brows crinkled with concentration. Although she did not say a word during the first few attempts, he could sense her frustration.

Stepping on his toes for the fourth time, she cried, "Oh, I am utterly hopeless."

Nigel stifled the moan of pain. "You are trying too hard. Don't fight the steps, just move with them."

"I can't. I am so worried about trampling on your toes…"

"You have managed that feat several times already. Let us try a different approach." His voice was a subtle blend of teasing and encouragement. He pulled her closer into him. "A waltz."

THE NEW POSITION felt so intimate, so… sensual.

"Let me guide you," his voice was low and seductive. "One… two… three… one… two…three." He continued to count in a soft rhythm as he guided through the elegant steps. She was dancing. Elation bubbled within. Not only was she dancing, but she also was not stepping on his toes!

The next half hour passed in absolute bliss. Nigel had been most attentive. When she'd confessed that she could not dance, without hesitation, he'd set about teaching her. Some of the hurt she'd felt had waned.

With graceful movements, he twirled her around the courtyard. His grip was firm on her waist, the movement of his body against hers arousing. The outside world faded into the distant shadows. A foreign tingling that had nothing to do with dancing started to arise from deep within. It was like nothing she had ever experienced before.

He guided her through another turn. Her world seemed to

tip upside down when his thigh brushed against her leg. She jumped back, bringing their waltz to an abrupt halt.

"I'm sorry… I…" She did not want him to know he had this effect on her. "I'm rather…" She could not find the words to finish her sentence, too embarrassed by the intimacy they'd just shared. Rather than embarrass herself further, she turned abruptly and ran away.

She had been enjoying his company. *Too much*, she thought, as she ran back into the house. It was dangerous for her to let her guard down. At any moment, the kindness and attention would end, and he would reveal his true purpose. With cruel words, he would break her heart once more. She wondered if she was strong enough to handle that heartache… again.

She was out of sorts and did not know what to do. She headed for the Green Parlor in the hope that her aunt had returned from her outing.

Walking into the parlor, she was relieved to find Aunt Lou taking afternoon tea. "How was your visit with Mrs. Hart?"

"Uneventful." Her relative waved for Artemisia to take the seat beside her on the settee. "I have a present for you, Arte."

She often told herself it did not matter if her aunt gave her presents or not, but she did always love the gifts Aunt Lou lavished on her. It was not that she needed or really wanted anything. It was just the thought that someone knew what she would like, not what she was expected to like.

Aunt Lou picked up a delicate brass bell and gave it several rings. A moment later, the footman arrived carrying a large white box, and placed it beside Artemisia. Her aunt smiled brightly and watched her with excitement.

Artemisia pulled the lid off, discarding it to one side. Pulling out a delicate dress with a blue satin lining covered by an overlay of ivory lace from the large box, she whispered, "It's beautiful." She looked at her aunt, whose eyes were beaming with delight.

"Do you like it?"

"Like it?" Tears stung the corner of her eyes. She choked on the words, "I love it. Where did you… how…?"

"It was to be a wedding gift. I had planned to give it to you when you arrived with Mr. Chartwick, but when…" her aunt stopped short, cleared her throat, then continued, "Well… whatever. I was waiting for the perfect time to give it to you."

"Why is now the perfect time?"

She watched Aunt Lou's mouth open to start a response when a knock sounded on the door. "Come in."

"Excuse the interruption, my lady. Lord Hawthorne has just arrived and will be joining you for dinner."

"Thank you, Simms."

"I believe I will rest awhile before dinner." And with that, her aunt took her leave, never answering Artemisia's question.

WHEN ARTEMISIA ENTERED the Yellow Dining Room with her aunt at her side, she could not remember a time in her life when she was more nervous. Every fiber of her being shook. She did not know how she was going to survive tonight. She was wearing the dress her aunt had given her earlier. She had been tempted to look in the mirror, but couldn't bring herself to. Instead, as usual, she'd relied on her lady's maid.

Maggie had assured her the dress was a perfect fit. But despite the maid's reassurances, Artemisia believed the dress to be too revealing. Even without having looked in her mirror, she was most conscious of the way the gown accentuated all her female curves. When Nigel eyed her up and down like a man long deprived, her fears were confirmed.

Glancing away from him in embarrassment, she was met with the arrival of Marcus.

"Marcus!" She could not contain her excitement, practically running into his open embrace. "It has been such a long time."

"Too long, little sprite." She had always loved that endearment. Although they were not related by blood, she felt a strong familial connection to Marcus. When she was with him, she felt like a little sister to his older brother. He had always watched out for her, and tormented and teased her, as only a big brother could. While other females would ogle his handsome features, honey-colored eyes, and dark blond hair, she adored him for his good heart and honesty.

Marcus pulled away from her embrace, empathy laced his features. "Lou informed me of what…?" His words suddenly halted. She noticed his surprise when he saw Nigel. "Nigel, what an unex—"

Nigel started coughing loudly into his fist. Artemisia watched as an unspoken communication passed between the two friends. It was just as she suspected. Nigel was not here to meet Marcus at Knollwood. So, why *was* he here?

Marcus tried to cover his faux pas. He stuttered out, "Oh… I hope I have not detained you from your other plans."

"On the contrary, I have had a most enjoyable visit with Lady Hawthorne and Miss Germayne." Nigel eyed Artemisia with a seductive smile. It was not the first time she'd been left breathless and puzzled. She did not like this game.

"Shall we dine?" Aunt Lou had a timetable to keep, especially when it came to meals. She was most particular that dinner was precisely at eight.

Aunt Lou presided at one end of the long table, Marcus at the other, while Artemisia sat on one side, with Nigel across from her. A large centerpiece of fresh roses partially blocked her view of him, but she could still sense his presence.

The liveried staff was in the midst of serving the meal when Aunt Lou began to question her nephew. "What news do you bring us from London?"

"The tittle-tatterers have been quite busy. In fact," Marcus started, and then sipped his wine, wanting to draw out the suspense of the information he had, as was his wont. Then, looking at Artemisia, he continued, "Most is centered on Rochefort here and your sister."

When Marcus looked her way, Artemisia could see the hidden question in his eyes. Could she deceive him the way she had deceived her aunt and Nigel?

She swallowed past the hard lump in her throat.

Aunt Lou raised a brow. "Harriet?"

"Philippa." Marcus stated matter-of-factly.

Nigel leaned to one side and peered at her from around the large centerpiece. His unnerving gaze never left her as Marcus shared the varying accounts. "There are rumors she is with child. Then there is the tale about how her lover…" Marcus stopped mid-sentence and pointed to Nigel with his thumb. "Left her for another, and she jumped into the Thames."

Artemisia started leaping from her seat at such false accusations. Tears stung her eyes. "She would never…"

"Of course she would not," Aunt Lou chimed in. She gave Artemisia the 'look'. *Stay calm, and don't let the words affect you.*

Marcus paid no attention to their protests. "And then, there is my favorite of all." The room fell silent in anticipation of the next outlandish statement. "That Nigel here,"

Marcus stopped and laughed before continuing, "murdered her. Is that not the most ridiculous accusation you've ever heard?"

Nigel gasped in shock. Aunt Lou huffed in disbelief. Artemisia just sat in pained silence, the weight of her role in this charade pulling her into the murky depths of despair. She was responsible for her sister's deception, which had now gone well beyond too far. She knew that distress was causing her heart to speed up and her fingers to tremble, but she could not calm her nerves.

Nigel was not responsible for her sister's disappearance, or even her elopement. Even before he'd told her to follow her heart, Philippa had made her mind up. She had only been looking for an excuse to ease her guilt, and Nigel had provided that. Now he was being accused by the gossips of murder?

"Are you alright, Arte?" Eyes unfocused, she heard the concern in her aunt's voice, but could not answer right away.

She began to stand, but her legs wobbled under the weight of her misguided conscience. Clutching the edge of the table, she managed to utter, "I...I think I am fatigued."

Head spinning in a daze over how much her falsehoods were affecting the people around her, she did not notice the others as she took her leave. A firm hand guided her down the hall, and up the grand staircase. When she stood in front of her bedroom door, a soft masculine voice whispered in her ear, "Get some rest, my love." The next thing she knew, Maggie was fussing over her.

CHAPTER 10

*M*arcus and Nigel had disappeared for most of the day, leaving Artemisia and Aunt Lou to enjoy each other's company.

Since it was just the two of them, her aunt seemed determined to discuss Artemisia's future prospects. "What do you intend to do once you return to London?"

Artemisia had been avoiding this topic ever since she'd arrived. She did not want to think about it, let alone discuss it out loud.

"I suppose Father will insist on finding me another match." She sighed and looked at her aunt, ready to confess her greatest fear. "The problem is, who will have me? It wasn't as if I was sought after before this scandal. Not to mention that *I* was the one left standing at the altar."

Aunt Lou started to laugh. "I see your point, dear Arte." Her voice was full of sarcasm as she continued, "You are not at all pretty, and have no interests, no accomplishments. You might as well be an ogre living under a bridge."

Matching her aunt's sarcasm, Artemisia corrected her. "I believe ogres live in caves. Trolls live under bridges." Her tone turned more serious as she tried to help her aunt see to reason. "You don't understand, Aunt Lou. I'm taller than most girls, my skin is too dark, I cannot dance, and I have curves that I am not sure any respectable female should have." She sighed heavily. "I'm just too different."

"You're unique. You have just not found that special someone." Her aunt's voice lightened. "And besides, men adore an ample bosom."

Artemisia glared at Lou. It was not a teasing matter. She had always been self-conscious about how she looked. She and her sisters were so unalike. They had never treated her differently, but she felt it just the same.

"And," her aunt's voice softened and filled with pride, "you have a beautiful singing voice, my dear."

My dear. Her aunt always resorted to that endearment when she was trying to make a specific point. Perhaps she did have more to offer than what met the eye.

"Would you like me to sing for you?"

"I thought you would never ask." Aunt Lou's smile warmed her heart.

NIGEL ENTERED the foyer and was taken aback by the faint sound that met his ears. Artemisia was singing.

He followed the sound of her sultry voice.

Standing to one side of the open door, so as not to be seen, he leaned against the wall and listened to the beautiful melody that flowed from her sensuous lips. He could not see her, but imagined her singing only to him. *Her long auburn hair swirling around her lush body, a seductive Italian love song, and eyes filled with passion.*

Lady Hawthorne's loud praise broke the spell. "That was most delightful, my dear."

He entered the parlor, expressing his admiration as well. "Absolutely beautiful."

Artemisia's chin dipped down and her cheeks reddened, as if she were embarrassed by the praise. Did she not truly know how accomplished she was?

Lady Hawthorne unexpectedly stood and announced, "I believe I have forgotten to write a letter to... a... someone," before scurrying from the room with much haste.

Nigel suspected what the old girl was up to and was thankful to have this moment alone with Artemisia.

Strolling to where she stood by the window, he showered her with praise. "You have a beautiful voice. Never shy away from it." He smiled until he saw the look on her face.

She was watching him with those crystal blue eyes, which were filled with years of hurt and pain—some of which he'd caused. How he regretted mocking her in his youth.

The hope in her voice nearly tore him apart. "*You* think I have a beautiful voice?"

He wanted to kiss away all her doubts. He would make up for his past wrongs every day for the rest of his life, as long as she was his.

"Did I miss anything?" Marcus said as he strolled into the parlor, clearly pleased with himself for interrupting their interlude.

Nigel grunted inwardly at the untimely appearance of his friend. Not only had Marcus chosen that moment to interrupt, but also had the audacity to narrow his gaze when he looked at Nigel.

Nigel knew Marcus was protective of Artemisia, but he felt like he was being sentenced to death before he'd committed the crime.

"Arte, would you care for a stroll in the garden?" Turning to Nigel, Marcus added for good measure, "You don't mind, do you?" The undertone of his voice suggested that he knew Nigel would very much indeed mind.

What was he supposed to say, *Yes, I do?* Nigel did not like playing *this* game. Artemisia belonged to him, and he did not want to share her.

"No, of course not," he acquiesced with reluctance.

WHEN ARTEMISIA TOOK the arm Marcus offered, she thought for a brief moment that Nigel would protest. His jaw was clenched, nostrils flared. The look on his face was one of controlled anger. The two were good friends, but there seemed to be an underlying tension. The three of them had spent much time together over the years and there had never been any friction before. What had changed as of late?

The stroll down to the garden was most pleasant. She had always enjoyed being out of doors on a day like this, especially at Knollwood. The cloudless sky was a brilliant shade of blue, the air warm and fragrant.

"Is he being a gentleman?" Marcus' question came out of nowhere, taking her aback for a moment.

"Yes, he is." At times, she wished Nigel wasn't. Their one brief kiss had been haunting her nights. She was curious about what would have happened if she had not been such a coward and rushed from the room.

Marcus paused on the pathway and eyed her. His expression suggested that he did not believe her.

"Why do you doubt his behavior?"

Marcus guided her to a shaded bench. When he turned to face her, she could see the concern on his face. "We have been partners in debauchery our entire lives. I know him better than you. I do not think someone can change so drastically because he has been isolated in the country for a week."

Shaking her head, not wanting to believe what Marcus was telling her, she argued. "Perhaps he has changed. Perhaps he enjoys being a gentleman. Perhaps the quiet country life suits him better than actresses, and… and the gaming hells of London. Perhaps…" She realized she had become most defensive of Nigel, much to Marcus' apparent entertainment.

Laughter encircled them. His eyes were bright with amusement. "Are you trying to convince me or yourself?" His mood quickly changed. He patted her hand and confessed, "You mean a great deal to me. I am just looking out for your best interests. I don't want to see you hurt by his actions."

LATER THAT DAY, too confined by her conflicting emotions, Artemisia decided to go for a long walk to clear her head. Before long, she was in the meadow, surrounded by white and yellow wildflowers, oblivious to the world happening all around her. Beautiful shades of pink filtered through the cloud-speckled sky. A westerly wind blew, carrying the scent of another day gone.

The conversation she'd had with Marcus had sent her hopes plummeting into despair. Was she reading too much into Nigel's actions, was he just trifling with her emotions, or had he changed? She walked through tall blades of grass in a haze of mixed emotions.

"I was hoping to find you alone."

The familiar, deeply masculine voice startled her back into the present. She turned around and found herself staring into Nigel's blue eyes.

Holding his hand out to her, he bowed slightly. His gaze

caressed her body and soul, tempting her. "May I have this dance?"

When she accepted his hand, he pulled her closer to him. He began to hum a melodious waltz, his voice low and seductive. The soft hum became a full orchestra in her mind as he guided her through the movements with gentle ease. She felt her body sway against his, keeping in time with the music.

The world around her became brighter. The wildflowers danced in the breeze. Sounds from nature accompanied their graceful movements, the meadow becoming their dance floor.

When we dance, my eyes see only you. When we dance, my body yearns for more. When we dance, everything seems possible. When we dance… I feel beautiful.

In that moment of clarity, she realized this was the greatest gift anyone had ever given her. And also, in that moment, she knew she had lost her heart to Nigel forever.

The thought terrified her.

CHAPTER 11

*L*ady Evans was throwing her annual summer ball. The crème de la crème descended on Evans Hall, one of the most impressive estates in the district, which boasted one hundred rooms, several ballrooms, an enormous hedge maze, and splendid orangery.

The Palladian-style mansion sat at the top of a large circular drive, glistening in the light of the full moon. The vastness of Lord and Lady Evans' wealth was apparent even before one entered the house. Once inside, the bright, candlelit entrance hall drew the guests towards a grand semi-circular staircase which led to the first of three ballrooms.

The largest ballroom was quite simple in its styling and décor. A series of pilasters on either side of the longest wall divided the space into equal compartments. Gilded framed mirrors reflected the sea of elegant dancers.

The second ballroom contained gaming tables, the third and smallest served as the refreshment hall. Each ballroom opened onto the large veranda, which overlooked a small lake, the gravel pathway to which was illuminated by hundreds of candles.

After they had been announced, Artemisia followed her aunt, who wanted to greet an old acquaintance. Marcus had excused himself and headed straight for the gaming room. All Nigel wanted to do was whisk Artemisia away from all these people. The moment she had descended the stairs at Knollwood, he'd known he would have a difficult time keeping his eyes—and hands—off her.

She was wearing a dress of soft violet satin ornamented with sprigs of silver, and her auburn hair was caught up in an elegant chignon with wavy tendrils cascading down her neck. He must have stared too long because Marcus muttered a warning that he pretended not to hear. Ever since that waltz in the meadow, he had thought of nothing else but her. The way she'd swayed against his body, her exotic scent, and her sweet dimples. How would he ever make it through this evening?

The quadrille had just ended, and couples were lining up for the next set. Nigel went to Artemisia's side without regard for the young buck standing next to her.

"May I have this dance?"

She did not say a word, but offered her hand. He led her onto the dance floor, her pulse quickening beneath his touch. He did not know if it was from the excitement of the occasion or his effect on her. He hoped it was the latter.

"Relax, and just enjoy yourself." Offering words of encouragement, he wanted her to take pleasure in the moment. When she smiled at him, he wished they were not on this crowded dance floor, but alone in his room. "You look beautiful," he whispered as the music began

Artemisia opened and closed her mouth, peering at him in disbelief.

Her steps were perfect. Only once did she falter. He squeezed her hand and softly counted the steps. Her crystal blue eyes were soft, like the sea on a calm day. She stared at him, he hoped, with the same desire he was feeling. He felt her breathing increase with each movement. When the dance ended and she stepped back, his body instantly regretted the loss.

No sooner had the set ended than Marcus approached them. "Artemisia, may I have the next dance?" His words broke their intimate interlude.

"Of course," she replied with enthusiasm.

Too much enthusiasm, in Nigel's opinion.

Nigel was certain that Marcus had asked Artemisia to dance just to annoy him. It had worked. Watching Marcus lead her through the movements of the set made his blood boil and jealousy overtook him. He clamped down his jaw and gritted his teeth in an attempt to ward off the not-so-unpleasant thought of confronting Marcus.

With each set she danced, Artemisia became more alive. She lit up the room with her dimples and bright smile. Nigel, in direct contrast, spent the entire evening festering in his own envy.

He watched her disappear out onto the terrace with Marcus. "Damn that bastard," he muttered under his breath. He wanted to pummel his fist into the first young buck that crossed his path.

With hands clenched tight, he moved through the crush, bumping into several couples. His destination was in sight. Turning to avoid two young ladies, he collided with a servant, who was carrying a tray of refreshments. Those around grunted with disgust at the mess. The glare from Lady Archibald, whose dress was the unfortunate victim of the accident, sent a shiver down his spine. The worst part was, by the time he reached the veranda, Marcus and Artemisia were nowhere to be seen.

.   .   .

THE CARRIAGE RIDE BACK to Knollwood was silent, except for Aunt Lou's gentle snoring, that is. Both Nigel and Marcus were simmering in opposite corners of the carriage. Artemisia did not know what had occurred to cause such friction between the two friends, but it was most disconcerting.

The two men glared at each other with yet more harshness. It seemed as if there was some secret competition going on between them. Ever since that day when she'd sung for her aunt, Marcus had tried his best to annoy Nigel. Whenever she was alone with Marcus, he treated her as he always did— like a little sister. But for reasons she could not fathom, he took great pleasure in annoying Nigel by implying there was more than met the eye with regard to her friendship with him. But her feelings for Marcus were very different from those she had for Nigel, who brought out all sorts of desires that she could not even begin to describe.

The well-sprung carriage rolled along at a casual pace. The wheels glided across the dark earth. Although it was only a short distance, the stress made the minutes drag on. It might as well have taken ten hours to return to Knollwood with all the roiling tension.

When the conveyance came to a halt, Aunt Lou popped her head up. "Home already? That was rather quick."

Artemisia had to stifle a giggle she suspected might be edged with a tinge of hysteria. It had seemed like the longest trip of her life, and she still had no idea why Nigel and Marcus were so angry with one another.

The steps were prepared, and the door opened, revealing Simms. "Good evening, my lady." Aunt Lou descended without words.

When at last all four of them had exited, Aunt Lou turned

to Marcus. Her tone held no emotion, no hint of what was to come. "I wish to speak with you privately in my room."

Taking his aunt's arm, Marcus guided her up the steps. When they reached the open door, he looked back over his shoulder at Artemisia. "Good evening, little sprite."

Artemisia was confused by the turn of events, and even more so when, after entering the hall, Nigel grasped her hand, and without a word, pulled her deeper into the house and the dark interior of the Green Parlor.

"What are you doing?" she whispered into the darkness.

The door clicked shut. Nigel turned to face her, his face illuminated by a faint stream of moonlight from the partially curtained window. One thing was for certain; he was angry.

"I could ask you the same thing," he whispered harshly.

Bewildered, she stared at him. "What is that supposed to mean?"

The rich colors of the room were already muted in the semi-darkness, and his mood foretold of something even darker. He strolled up to her, only a breath away. "Why did you flirt with every young buck tonight?"

Stunned, Artemisia did not answer because she had no idea who he was even referring to.

Nigel, however, did not lack for words. "What did you discuss with Marcus this evening on the veranda? Where did you go with him? Did he take you to the grotto?"

"Why are you acting like this?" Artemisia's voice quavered. He was ruining her first successful social event. "First, you tell me that you want me to live, to enjoy life. Then, when I finally take that chance, you harass me. You are impossible." Her voice rose in anger, and her body trembled with rage. "You are selfish and… and impossible. You only think of yourself and what you want. For the first time in my life, I did not sit on the outskirts waiting… hoping. You gave me such a wonderful gift in teaching me to dance, and now you stand there trying to take it all away from me."

NIGEL FROWNED AT HER. Artemisia was furious with him. Again. How could she think him insincere? He was protecting her from a thoughtless rogue.

Rage consumed him as she defended his former best friend. "Marcus has been nothing but a gentleman. He is like a brother to me. And besides, he is not the rake you make him out to be."

He should show her just what a rake did. Without further thought, he pulled her into him. Artemisia's eyes flashed with the same desire that coursed through him. All thoughts of punishing her went by the wayside. She might later deny it, but he could see her hunger.

He bent his head and took her lips in a soft, yet demanding kiss, caressing them, begging her to open to his demands. He felt like a beggar. He wanted more, so much more. With each sigh of pleasure, Artemisia teased and tormented him. He could not get enough of her. He was quickly losing control.

She must have felt the same. Her hands explored his chest, and then travelled up to the nape of his neck. He felt her nails scratch at the exposed skin at the base of his neck. Desire shot through him. In one fell swoop, he picked her up in his arms and carried her to the settee. Sitting down with her in his lap, he began his own slow exploration.

Pressing light, openmouthed kisses down the column of her neck only made him want more. She tasted like springtime after a cool rain, fresh and intoxicating.

When she gasped, he took her mouth in a harder kiss, entangling his tongue with hers. Her bottom shifted, sending waves of desire through his lower limbs. He wanted to take her right here, right now.

He pulled back and looked into her passion-filled eyes. He was most certain that she had never been in a situation like this before. Delighted with the thought, he nibbled her lips.

Breathing in deep, he rested his head against hers and let out a long sigh. "This is not a good idea," he murmured under his breath. He heard her gasp and felt her begin to pull away. He kept her firmly against him. Not wanting her to misunderstand his intentions, he clarified, "I want you more than you could possibly realize."

"Oh…" The sweet sound held a host of meanings—hope, desire, temptation.

Brushing his hand across her cheek, he silenced her with a kiss that was meant to be one of reassurance. She matched his ardor, and the kiss turned heated, sensuous, and in only a matter of moments. This was what he had dreamt about for weeks; years, if he was honest with himself.

Between labored breaths, he heard a noise come from outside the parlor door. She must have heard it, too, because she jumped off his lap, grabbed his hand and pulled him to the opposite side of the room.

"What…?"

She silenced him with a quick kiss, and then whispered, "There is a secret door."

His little siren was becoming quite resourceful. It was too dark for him to make out what she was doing, but he heard a soft click, then felt a chilly breeze. She tugged for him to follow.

Winding their way through a hidden passage, he uttered a silent prayer that they would not be caught. He fully intended to marry Artemisia, but wanted to do it properly. They emerged into the dark night. The outside air was like a splash of cold water on his face.

Somewhat regaining his senses, he declared, "I believe it is for the best if I say good night." He turned and left a bewildered—and far too desirable—Artemisia.

CHAPTER 12

*D*espite the very satisfying kiss he had shared with Artemisia, Nigel had not forgotten the matter of Philippa's disappearance, or the scandalous gossip that was still running rampant through the *ton*. Or the note Artemisia had dropped. It was time he learned what she knew.

Artemisia and Lady Hawthorne had traveled into the village for the day to shop, and Marcus had gone off for a ride. The house was empty, save for the servants. After learning that Maggie, Artemisia's maid, was enjoying an afternoon off, Nigel took the opportunity to investigate Artemisia's room.

The White Room, which Artemisia occupied, was in fact decorated in varying shades of lavender. It was extremely tidy. He suspected that even without a lady's maid, Artemisia would be neat. Nigel moved throughout the room, careful not to disrupt anything. Her scent lingered in the air, momentarily distracting him from his mission.

A simple writing desk in dark mahogany graced a well-lit spot by the open window. He approached, pulling one drawer out, then the other. He thought it odd that both were empty.

Upon closer inspection, he realized the second drawer was not as deep as the first.

Perhaps there was a secret compartment. Stretching his hand farther back, he felt for a latch. None was to be found. He started to withdraw his hand when his sleeve caught on something.

Pulling back his arm, he was fumbling to release his sleeve when he felt a very small, round knob. It did not open outwards, but rather slid across to the side. He strained to reach farther into the compartment again. A sheet of paper lifted beneath his fingers. The opening was small, and he struggled to release the folded sheets, but with a little patience, he eventually extracted three small scraps of paper.

Before reading the notes, he felt again for any more. Satisfied that the compartment was empty, he moved closer to the window.

My dearest love,

All is set for our departure. I am counting the seconds until we are reunited and become one. My soul is aflame with desire for you.

Your eternal love,

A.K.

Nigel was disgusted with what he saw. How could Artemisia be in love with such a sap? He read the next letter, which was even more nauseating than the first.

My darling dove,

My body longs for yours. I cannot wait to taste you once again. Your sweetness haunts me when we are apart. Only one more day and we will be joined together.

Forever yours,

A.K.

It was decided. He was going to kill whoever A.K. was. Was it possible that *A.K.* had ruined Artemisia and left her?

His blood was at a boiling point when he began the last of the three notes he'd discovered.

My pretty Philly,
I will come for you when the house stills.
Your soon-to-be…
A.K.

Philly? Could these love letters have belonged to Philippa?

Was the note Artemisia had dropped part of the scheme? Instead of discovering answers, he had more questions. He'd underestimated the lengths Artemisia was willing to go to in order to protect her sister. He was certain she was hiding something from him. Her behavior had been very odd whenever he'd mentioned Philippa.

Although the letters, and why Artemisia was in possession of them, confused him, he was confident now that Artemisia did not have a secret lover. She was too unpracticed and naïve. He should have been relieved; but one question still plagued him. What other secrets *did* she have?

THE HOUR WAS LATE, the entire house was still, and yet, Nigel could not rest. He had spent the last hour pacing, trying to decide what to do about Artemisia. He knew she was keeping something from him; she had been avoiding him ever since she'd returned from her outing. One more circuit of the room decided it—he would go to her room and demand answers.

He stepped out into the dark hallway. Not a soul in sight, or noise to be heard. He walked the short distance to her bedroom and pressed his ear to the door for any sound of movement, not willing to disturb her if she was already asleep.

Thoughts of interrogation drifted into the recesses of his mind when he heard her most seductive voice singing in Italian. The sound melted his heart. It was as if she was singing just for him. He hated to disrupt this most glorious song, but there were matters which needed to be discussed.

When he tapped on the door, the singing instantly stopped. He heard movement on the other side and waited anxiously as the seconds dragged on. He clenched his teeth, trying to control the urge to pound on the door.

When it finally edged open, he was rewarded with the sight of his beautiful siren clad in white.

Artemisia's blue eyes looked at him in question. "Nigel," she started, glancing both ways down the hall, "what are you doing here?"

"I need to know what happened to your sister."

"I don't… I don't know any more than you."

He suspected she knew more than she was letting on. Her manner was most peculiar. "I think you do. Why else would you be worrying the edge of your dressing gown?"

Although she spoke in hushed tones, her voice was firm. "Because it is the middle of the night, and you are standing outside my bedroom door."

As much as Nigel hated to admit it, her reason was valid.

She was far too enticing by half. Her long auburn hair cascaded about her waist and her white dressing gown caressed her glowing skin. In one swift movement, he could have her inside and naked on the bed. He stood for long moments before reality hit him like a wave crashing upon the land.

Artemisia continued to eye him with uncertainty.

He did not want to leave, but he also did not want to be caught in a compromising situation. His plan was to court her, possibly seduce her a little, and then marry her, in that order.

Stroking her smooth cheek, he leaned in and took her mouth in a sensuous kiss. She did not gasp as on previous occasions, and did not protest, although she should have. The kiss was so intoxicating he did not want it to end. It took tremendous willpower not to have his way with her.

Pulling back, his heart was pounding hard from restraint, his breath a quick staccato. He should give her an explanation, or at least apologize for his lack of manners. In the end, all he could manage was a polite salutation. "Goodnight, my love."

WHAT WAS he doing at her door? This was most inappropriate. And yet, Artemisia found the idea of Nigel coming to her during the night more than appealing.

But when he started questioning her about Philippa, she did not know what to say. So, she blurted out the first thing that came to mind. "I don't... I don't know any more than you."

It was a lie, of course. She knew exactly what had happened to Philippa. She'd eloped with Mr. Alfred Keates, her one true love. Keates shared Philippa's adoration of horses, and she shared his desire to build the most famous stable in all of England.

Artemisia did not want to lie to Nigel. She knew how he valued honesty above all else. She was torn between telling him everything and betraying her sister's trust, or lying to him and risk losing him forever. The problem was, she did not know what his intentions were.

Her conscience continued to tell her he was playing some sort of game. He had not asked for her hand, or even declared his undying love and affection for her. Despite all that had happened between them, she still did not think it possible that he would even be interested in someone like her. Perhaps he was only using her to clear his name of scandal.

And then he'd kissed her. When his lips had met hers, she'd thought she would melt on the spot. Her flimsy dressing gown had been no barrier for the heat that she felt. She knew she should have protested. A proper young lady of the *ton* would have. But she was tired of being a proper young lady. She wanted to experience all the emotion and desire that had caused her sister to throw caution to the wind and elope with Mr. Keates.

When Nigel thrust his tongue into her mouth, she had not gasped, but met his desire with her own. Having his body so close to hers had been sublime. No sooner had the kiss begun than it had ended. She was ashamed to admit that she wanted more. What *more* was entailed, she was unsure. All she knew was that her body ached for his touch.

"Good night, my love," was the last thing she'd heard before Nigel had crossed the hall and disappeared into his room.

She closed her door and felt as if she glided across the room and floated down onto her soft feather bed. She sighed with joy, "My love."

CHAPTER 13

The next day started out as one of the happiest that Artemisia could ever recall. Nigel had called her *my love*. It was a sure sign that he felt more than just a passing fancy for her. She could not stop smiling, so giddy with delight was she over those two words, her mood could not be dampened.

By that afternoon, she was lost in a world of her own, still overcome with joy. Wanting to impress Nigel the next time they danced, she decided to practice.

She pushed open the wide double doors that led into the ballroom and found the room was dark and cold from disuse. The soft tap of her shoes echoed as she crossed the vast parquet floor toward the windows. With methodic ease, she pulled several sets of curtains open, allowing the afternoon light to filter into the cream and gold space.

Holding out her arms as if dancing a waltz, she began to move while counting. "One, two, three… one, two, three…"

She twirled around a corner and came face to face with Nigel. Without missing a step, he put one hand on the small of her back, and with the other, took her hand in his. She felt her heartbeat quicken at his touch as they moved through the ballroom on a cloud of desire.

One moment he was twirling her around, the next, he had her pressed up against the wall and was kissing her senseless, his lips demanding and perfect.

His hands were everywhere, begging for her to open to him. Any decent young lady would have stopped him the moment his hand had cupped her breast. But Artemisia did not. She was curious, and her body screamed with a want she did not understand. The current onslaught of his attention was most invigorating. She pressed herself closer to him, desperate for more.

"Artemisia." She heard him whisper through the haze of her desire. Just the thought that he could not control himself any more than she could excited her beyond imagination.

But the reality of where they were, and of who could walk in at any moment, was like a bucket of cold water on her face. "This isn't proper," she managed to mutter between kisses.

His response was a guttural growl of frustration.

She pulled back and looked into his eyes. She could see the passion and honesty in thems. There were no lies, no secrets, just mutual longing. Years of heartache washed away in that moment.

He took several steps back, cleared his throat, and proceeded to say in a formal tone that held none of the passion they just shared, "Thank you for the dance." Squaring his shoulders, he turned on his heel and left her standing alone.

His tone and manner had changed so quickly, Artemisia was thoroughly confused, not knowing what she had done wrong. Was he upset because she'd halted their passion? Had he not experienced the same breathlessness as her? Skulking out of the ballroom, paying no heed to where she was walking, she bumped right into her aunt.

"You look rather spent, Arte. Are you unwell?"

"I *am* feeling rather tired." She did not want to tell her aunt the truth. *I've just been ravished by Nigel, and then he walked out of the room.* No, that would not do. Her aunt would be furious with him if Marcus did not kill him with pistols at dawn first.

"Why don't you retire early." It was not a question, but more of a gentle command. "I will have supper sent to your room."

"Thank you, I think I will." Artemisia kissed her aunt and began to walk toward the grand staircase. She ran her warm hand across the smooth, cool railing and then brought it to her feverish cheeks. What had she done?

By the time she reached her room, she was ready for a night of peace and quiet.

HE HAD JUST BEEN KISSING Artemisia in the ballroom, where anyone could have walked in and seen them. If Marcus had found out, he would have challenged him. He did not need that scandal hanging over his head. He wanted to court her properly, he reminded himself. But every time they were near each other, Nigel lost all thought and reason, and instead felt an insane desire to have her in his arms.

After wandering the grounds for an hour, kicking up dust like he was five years old, he was no less content with the situation. He was making a complete ass of himself whenever he was near Artemisia.

Entering the primary courtyard, he was surprised to discover Lady Hawthorne tending to the roses. Most ladies of the *ton* would never be seen on their knees performing such a menial task as pulling weeds.

"Good afternoon," he greeted her with a smile that he did not feel. "It's a nice afternoon." His attempt at small talk was… small.

"Oh, it has been a most pleasant afternoon, and promises to be an even more pleasant evening." Lady Hawthorne paused a moment. Perhaps he only imagined it, but Nigel thought he saw a mischievous flash in her eye. "If only Artemisia wasn't unwell."

Artemisia was ill? He'd seen her only an hour ago, and she was hail then. Perhaps their encounter had distressed her. "What seems to be the matter?"

Waving a small spade, Lady Hawthorne responded with nonchalance, "I'm sure she is fine. Just overexerted herself, I suppose. She looked flushed and red all over. Perhaps I am just overly concerned…."

Nigel listened while Lady Hawthorne rambled on and on… and on. Not wanting to interrupt, but not wanting to spend what was left of the afternoon listening to her meanderings, he changed the subject and asked, "Will dinner be at eight?"

"I suppose." Lady Hawthorne's response came out slowly and with reluctance. "It will be rather awkward with just the two of us."

"Two of us? You mean just you and me?"

Tending to one stubborn weed, she nodded her head. "Marcus has gone to town, and I don't expect him back till late, and Arte is to take her meal in her room." She glanced up from her task and teased, "If you don't think me a poor hostess, then I think I shall dine in my room as well." Turning her attention back to the weed, she yanked hard. "I am getting too old for this sort of work, but I do love my roses. They bring me such joy, and they're so fragrant, and have such beautiful…."

Nigel did not know if it was a ploy to scare him off, or if Lady Hawthorne had, in fact, advanced to an age where rambling on about nothing at all for considerable lengths of time was the norm. Wanting to make a quick escape, he released himself. "I believe a quiet evening is in order. If you will excuse me, I will retire as well."

It was a flimsy response. Regardless of how fond he was of the old girl, he was not in the mood to listen to the constant wandering and opinions of Lady Hawthorne for an entire evening. As he walked away, he thought he heard her chuckle.

Not wandering at all. What a sly old fox she was, he thought to himself with a smile.

After departing Lady Hawthorne's company, he walked about the gardens and then retired to his room. If he were in residence at Kettleworth, he would have had no problem filling his evening. There was always some business to attend to on the estate. He missed his home and the sense of purpose he felt while there.

Day had given way to night. The evening crept by one slow second at a time. He felt like a caged animal, scratching at the bars, begging for escape. Restlessness consumed his every breath.

Had Artemisia's illness been caused by what had happened in the ballroom earlier that day? He paced the length of his room, stopping in front of the large window for the umpteenth time. Bright stars flickered against the black sky; perhaps another walk around the grounds would ease his conscience. But then again…

He continued to pace, wondering if Artemisia had a

headache. He completed another circle. Perhaps she had a fever. On the next pass, he became most certain that he recalled hearing of an outbreak of smallpox in the next village. No, it could not possibly be smallpox, but perhaps, a common cold.

He convinced himself that he needed to make sure Artemisia had not taken a turn for the worse. The list of ailments that she could have contracted was growing with each turn he made.

The house had quieted. He strolled across the hall and tested the handle of her bedroom. It wasn't locked. If she was asleep, he would not wake her, only glance in to know that she was not suffering through a megrim, or the smallpox, or...

He stepped inside and closed the door. Several candle-sticks lighted the room, and the scent of lavender hung in the air. Artemisia was not in bed, but was standing at the window, brushing her long hair, and humming softly into the night. Should he go?

The decision was made for him when she turned around. Her eyes shone with question and curiosity. Relief coursed through him. She wasn't ill.

As she walked toward him, past the vanity, he noticed a covering draped over the mirror. He did not have to time to wrap his mind around that conundrum. There were more important activities to explore. In three strides, he'd covered the space between them and was kissing her.

This was what he wanted, what he longed for.

He nibbled her earlobe. "You taste like forbidden fruit." She giggled in his arms at his declaration. She felt like a warm summer day. "You are so beautiful."

She stiffened with those words. Pulling back, he looked into her opulent eyes. The pain he had witnessed previously had crept its way back. "Do you not know how beautiful you are?"

"I… I." She let out a long sigh. "I don't know what I look like, I…I stopped looking in the mirror years ago." Her words struck a chord with him. Why would she not want to gaze upon herself? Did she not…

Wait a moment.

Was that why the mirror was covered? She tried to turn her head away, but he cupped her cheek with his hand. Holding her firmly against him, giving her no opportunity to run, he questioned, "Why is that?"

Tears were beginning to pool in the corner of her eyes. "B…because of what… someone said."

"Who would say…?" His words died as she finished his sentence.

"You."

Her confession tore at his insides, and his heart plummeted with the heavy weight of his thoughtless words and actions he had caused her through the years. But he would make amends for his past wrongs. Taking her by the hand, he led her towards the full-length mirror that was also covered. She tried to pull her hand free, but he gently kept it within his grasp.

She stood with her back to the mirror, her body visibly tense with fear that something horrible was about to happen. It might as well have been a firing squad for the look she gave him. Moving around her, he reached to pull the cloth off the mirror.

When he faced her again, her eyes were closed tight. "I don't want to look." He turned her towards the mirror, as she pleaded, "Please don't make me look." She was trembling from head to toe.

He stood behind her, feeling the heat from her body as it

radiated from her. "You are so beautiful it makes me ache." He ran a finger down the column of her neck, across her shoulder and down her arm. He took her trembling hand in his and then, in a soft and gentle voice, he said, "Look in the mirror."

She shook her head, keeping her eyes shut.

With his other hand, he began to undo the tie at the top of her nightgown.

"What are you doing?" Her voice was quiet, unsure.

"I want you to see how desirable you are. I want to…" His heavy sigh was laced with years of regret. "I'm sorry for all the hurtful words I have spoken. You once told me that I was selfish…."

Artemisia's eyes flew open as she began to protest. "I did not…"

His eyes locked with hers in the mirror. "You were right. Whenever I did not get my way, I said cruel things that I would not normally say."

I was jealous of Chartwick. I did not want him to have what I could not. I arranged for him to escape to the country. I did not understand what I was feeling then, but I do now, is what he should have confessed. He wanted her to realize what he'd done was for her own good, for their future, not for Chartwick or any other, but for them.

Instead, he settled for the first thought that came to mind. "You belong to me."

When Nigel declared that she belonged to him, her heart leapt with excitement. A part of her that she had not known existed came to life. Nigel was standing so close behind her. The position was arousing, seductive. His breath coursed down her spine, sending with it a delicious shiver of anticipation. She could hardly think straight while he kissed her neck, and his hand roamed over a taut nipple. She should stop him. She should ask him to leave. But she didn't want to. She wanted this more than it made sense to deny.

Throwing caution to the wind, she whispered with a shyness that she hoped didn't sound too naïve, "Make love to me."

His response came not in words, but in actions. In one swift movement, he lifted her nightgown off her body and flung it into the darkness. Turning her head away from the mirror, she opened her eyes and focused on a candle burning on the mantel. She did not want this moment to be destroyed by the sight of her own naked image.

Nigel's firm but gentle hand turned her head back. His voice was low and seductive, sending another a delicious shiver down her spine. "I want you to watch me pleasure you."

Her body heated with those words. She stared with curiosity, keeping her gaze on Nigel's fingers as he began to caress the column of her neck, moving lower across her chest.

Everywhere he touched tingled with new life. Her chest rose and fell rapidly in anticipation of what was next to come.

"Look in the mirror. Look at yourself." For the first time in years, Artemisia did not fear what she might see.

Artemisia gazed at her reflection. Her skin was not as dark as she remembered, her curves not as severe. Her long auburn hair cascaded about her waist, framing her taut stomach.

Nigel stood behind her, doing incredible things to her body. He kissed her ear, then nibbled the column of her neck, taking in deep breaths. "You smell like lavender on a summer's night."

She watched as one masculine finger circled around her

hardened nipple. She had no idea that such a simple touch could create such a torrent of yearning.

"Your skin is smooth as velvet." Relaxing into him, she relished the sensation of his strong form behind her. His words aroused her, and his touch inflamed her. She continued to watch his fingers create intricate patterns across her breast, traveling down her abdomen, past her navel.

She gasped in shock when he neared her femininity. "Nigel, I…"

Kissing her neck, she felt his words skim over her heated skin. "Shh, my love." Her knees wobbled, but he held her firm against him, one hand splayed across her stomach, while the other cupped her mons. When one long finger entered her most delicate folds, she thought she would faint from the pleasure.

"Oh, my…" Her head flung back, her breath coming in short spurts. "What are…?"

"Just relax and watch."

She felt… naughty. There was no other word for it. She watched his finger disappear into her curls, desire and excitement rising with each thrust. When he pulled it out, she felt a momentary loss. She edged closer to his hand, wanting him to push his finger inside once more, find that delicate spot.

"You are beyond alluring, my siren."

Glancing over her shoulder, she looked into his blue eyes and saw her future. She was no longer afraid, or hesitant. Turning to face him, she wrapped her arms around his neck and kissed him with all the love, desire, and passion that she felt. This is where she longed to be. This is where she belonged.

.   .   .

His siren was undoing any measure of self-control Nigel thought he had. He'd meant to go slowly, take his time, and savor the moment. But when she turned into him and kissed him, there was no turning back.

Scooping her up into his arms, he carried her the short distance to her bed. Placing her on it, his body throbbing with the need to have her naked beneath him, he tore his clothes off in a frenzy of want. She watched him with curiosity.

Standing at the foot of the bed, he began to caress her feet, his eyes gliding over her splendid body. Her round hips and voluptuous bosom were made for seduction.

Her voice quavered. "Why are you staring?"

"You are so beautiful." He did not know what to say to convince her. "I want to explore every inch of your perfect form." With each compliment he showered, her smile began to build. He did not know how long he could stave off his own desire when she looked at him with eyes shining and full of hunger.

Lifting one delicate foot to his mouth, he showered kisses along its top, and then kissed his way up her leg. When he reached the juncture between her thighs, she gasped and tried to edge away. He held her to the bed with a firm hand, while the other parted her delicate, moist folds. He bent his head and took her sweet flesh in his mouth. A delicious moan escaped her when he flicked his tongue across her sensitive bud.

"Oh… Oh, my."

That was all the encouragement he needed. He thrust his tongue into her again and again, savoring the taste of her. *You're mine*, echoed through his head as he lapped the sensitive nub.

He heard her moan and knew her climax was near. He

delved his tongue into her sweetness once more and sucked harder. He would never have his fill of her.

A brief moment later, her body bucked in climax. "That was…"

"Just the beginning."

Pressing kisses along her heated flesh, he caressed his way up her body. He could hear her heart beating loudly, her breathing increasing with each kiss and nibble.

He wanted her more than he had ever wanted another woman, and this time, for the first time in his life, he did not take precautions against an unwanted child. He had always been most careful in that regard. He knew too many that had been labeled 'bastards' because of their fathers' negligence. He did not want that guilt hanging over his head. But tonight, it was different. Artemisia was different. She was his.

When he slid his throbbing member into her wet shaft, he thought he would spill himself right then and there. He had never made love to a woman without the use of French letters, and it felt… divine. Artemisia, naked beneath him, was better than anything he could have ever imagined. There was a moment's hesitation when he came to her barrier because he did not want to cause her pain.

Looking down into her clear blue eyes, he whispered, "This may hurt."

"I trust you." Her words touched him like none other.

Without so much as a warning, he broke through her innocence. She stiffened, her nails digging into his neck, her breathing heavy. He whispered words of endearment while bringing her to new heights of pleasure. He continued to plunge into her slickness until she found her peak. Unable to control his appetite, he pounded again against her quivering flesh, finding his own release a moment later.

Their breath intermingled in the aftermath of their love-making, Nigel rolled to one side, bringing Artemisia with him. He did not want the moment to end. Cradling her in his arms, he showered kisses on her temple. Her soft smile and sweet dimples spoke volumes. The rhythm of her breathing slowed as she drifted off to sleep. Before too long, he gave into slumber, entwined in her embrace.

CHAPTER 14

*T*he air was warm and filled with the scent of blossoms. The extensive flower garden with its intricate rose lined pathways was an exotic intoxication on her senses. All the joy Artemisia felt bubbled to the surface. She could not contain her smile, nor did she want to.

For the first time in her three and twenty years, she felt beautiful. It wasn't just on the outside, either. When Nigel looked at her, he saw *her*. He knew her flaws, and yet, when she looked into his eyes, she saw desire, caring, and understanding. It both excited and scared her.

She worried that, with time, Nigel might grow tired of her. He was, after all, a rake. He could have his pick of women. He wanted her now, but how long would it last?

And then, there was still the matter of her sister. She wanted to trust Nigel, but it was not her secret to reveal. Besides, Philippa would be returning soon, and the *ton* would learn that Nigel had had nothing to do with Philippa's elopement. Artemisia hoped she would have her happily ever after, too. Then her world would be perfect.

Walking over to a rosebush that her aunt had planted only

last year, she leaned in to smell the fragrant blossoms. The sweet perfume permeated her mind. Thoughts of Nigel warmed her insides, creating a yearning that she still did not quite understand. But then, her most pleasant reflections were interrupted by the sound of footsteps crunching in the gravel behind her.

A soft, deep, masculine voice penetrated her soul. "Artemisia."

She turned around, expecting to see Nigel's passion and ardor. Instead, his features were troubled, grief stricken. *He'd discovered her secret.*

"Before you become angry, just listen." His words were lined with remorse.

It was worse than she'd assumed. Her insides went cold at those words. Her world began to tilt. Nigel was going to tell her that last night was a mistake.

The words rushed from Nigel's mouth, "Chartwick confided that he did not love you the way a fiancé should. He was marrying you for your dowry, to clear his father's debt." He ran a hand through his blond hair. Staring at the ground, he continued, "I gave him the means so he would not have to marry you."

She felt as if the ground had dropped out beneath her. It *was* worse than she had thought. It had all been a game to him. Tears began to sting the corner of her eyes. She thought her voice would give way before she even had a chance to form the words. "W…was it Chartwick's idea or… or y… yours to humiliate me in front of the *ton*?"

"That was not the original intent."

It may have not been his intent, but it had been the result. "You have done and said some cruel things, but this…" Her voice wavered with emotion. "…this is too low…" She did not want to let him see her cry. She sucked in her breath, fighting back the tears. "Just let me alone and leave Knollwood."

Not waiting for a response, she started to storm past him when his firm hand caught her arm and swung her into him. He held her tight against his chest, giving her no opportunity to pull away.

His voice rumbled, penetrating to the depths of her soul. "I will not leave Knollwood, and I will not leave you."

His lips brushed her ear. In spite of all he had done, his hot breath sent delightful shivers down her spine. She detested the way her body gave into his touch and still craved more. The hatred and humiliation that had been consuming her began to fade with the stroke of his fingers. His firm body next to hers clouded her senses and left her speechless.

He continued to hold her tight against him. Her body warmed with each breath she took. When his words came, they were soft and caring, full of remorse. "Artemisia, forgive me."

Embarrassed and confused, she could not manage to put even two simple words together. "I…I…" She pushed out of his embrace and ran off. The tears she'd barely held in check in front of him started to stream down her face.

She needed room to breathe. To think. She had always suspected that Nigel had had something to do with Chartwick's lack of commitment, but now it was confirmed. She wanted to be angry with Nigel, but deep down, despite the humiliation, she was thankful. She would not have been happy with Chartwick. In fact, she is most certain they would have made each other miserable over the years. She was embarrassed by how easy it was to forgive Nigel for something that had caused her so much grief only a short time ago.

She hurried through the house and out into the center

courtyard. The Great Oak had always offered quiet solitude and comfort in the past. Today was the exception.

She was not surprised when she saw Nigel approaching with caution. She had known that he would follow, but she needed a moment to regain her composure.

"I thought I would find you here." Before she had a chance to speak, he closed the distance between them. "I don't want to argue. I know what I did was wrong, but…"

Her voice quavered with each word. "You humiliated me in the church… in front of my family and… I was angry…."

"I realized that the moment you punched me." He rubbed the spot on his jaw where she had struck him.

Remembering his shocked expression on what was supposed to be her wedding day, she could not prevent the smile that crept across her face. "I couldn't help myself. You sat there looking so smug and…"

He took a step closer.

Even before that disastrous day, her life had been consumed with strife. She was tired of fighting and arguing. She wanted love and passion, and… She knew what she had to do.

"I forgive you," she whispered with all the love she felt, but had not been ready to speak. No matter what the future held, she could not wither under anger.

"You do?" The surprise in his voice almost made her laugh. "Why?"

"I wasn't in love with Chartwick. I just wanted…" She did not want to confess what she'd hoped for, afraid that he did not want the same thing as her. Leaning against the rough tree trunk, she gazed up into the oak's branches that seemed to hold the secret desires of those who'd gone before her.

"I'm curious about something." She lowered her gaze,

meeting his lovely blue eyes. "You once told me the story about the initials on this tree."

"Yes, I remember. I was annoyed with you for being here and…"

Her skin tingled when he brushed a soft kiss on her cheek. "Am I still not welcome?"

"You most certainly are." The words dragged out of her mouth as her breathing increased with the nearness of him, the memory of what they had shared still fresh in her mind. "You were going to ask me something?" She really did not want to lose the moment, but they were in plain view of several rooms in the house.

"The initials…" He kissed the tip of her nose, before continuing, "Who do they belong to?" He kissed her forehead, then her temple.

"I do not remember," she replied in bewilderment. She was so mesmerized by him, his closeness, that at that moment, if someone had asked her name, she was not sure she could have answered.

He kissed her cheek. "I think I know."

Too nervous to ask, she began to worry her bottom lip.

"What's wrong?"

Only moments ago, he'd confessed his wrongdoing. It was time for her to speak of at least some of the things that were on her mind. She kicked some pebbles about, not making eye contact. "I worry that you might tire of me."

Nigel took her hands in his. "I will not ever tire of you. I only want you." Turning to stare into his eyes, she saw the sincerity when he spoke, but still could not believe that he wanted her.

"You could have your pick of women…."

"Did you not hear what I said? I don't want another

woman. I only want *you*. Not for a day, not for a life, but for eternity."

Years of pent-up emotions surfaced. Choking on her word, she cried, "Why?" She did not understand how someone as handsome as Nigel could want someone as different as herself.

"You're beautiful, and intelligent, and have the voice of an angel. You make me want to be a better man. You are thoughtful and sincere, and more passionate than you realize."

He thought she was beautiful and passionate? He had said the words before, but today she *believed* that he meant them. "You are not bothered by my looks?"

A soft chuckle rumbled in his chest. "Bothered? I am obsessed." He ran his hand up the column of her neck, then cupped her cheek. "Your skin looks like it has been kissed by the sun." He kissed her cheek. "Your eyes are more brilliant than a thousand diamonds floating on the open sea." He kissed her forehead. "Your breasts were made for my hands to fondle. Your lips were made for pleasure." He took her mouth in a kiss that made her toes curl.

She leaned into his masculine form as desire shot down the length of her. His right hand rested on her back, the other still holding her hand. *One, two, three…* He began to guide her through the steps of a waltz.

She hummed the *Slow Waltz*. Hands touching, he guided her through graceful movements, in perpetual circles. He lifted his left hand, keeping hers within his, sweeping her beneath their outstretched arms. When she came full circle, their eyes met. Mutual desire shone deep within. She could hardly control her breathing; she was only beginning to understand their passion.

"I think it is best if we end today's lesson." Nigel's voice was heavy with desire, and it thrilled her.

NIGEL HAD NOT WANTED the waltz to end, but he certainly could not make love to Artemisia in broad daylight in the center courtyard. Lady Hawthorne, or worse, Marcus, was bound to discover them. With much reluctance, they had gone their separate ways. However, he was already planning his next dance of seduction. In the meantime, he needed to find a diversion for his mind and hands, or he would go insane with anticipation of their next *rendezvous*.

He had always enjoyed working with his hands. It gave him purpose. When he was a young boy, he remembered having been envious of the stablemen. They had a useful occupation. Their days were not filled with the endless boredom of rules and regulations. By the time he'd reached adulthood, he'd realized that everyone was governed by the rules placed upon them by society and their particular class. He knew he was of the privileged class, but still envied the work that occupied the stablemen's days.

Whenever he'd been frustrated or upset or had a row with his father—which was quite often, he could always be found in the stables. He loved the feel of horseflesh, the raw power combined with a smooth, luxurious coat. The scent of fresh hay was a soothing balm. Through the years, none of this had changed.

Driving the pitchfork into the hay, he lifted the heavy load to toss aside when his ritual was interrupted.

"Thought I would find you out here." Marcus' smug voice rose above the sound of the horses' hooves and whinnies. "You are quite predictable."

"What do you want?" Nigel growled with frustration and

annoyance. Ever since the night of Lady Evans' ball, they had
been at odds with each other.

Marcus leaned against a wood panel and began to inspect
his hand before speaking. "I came to discuss Artemisia."

"Why?"

"I want to ensure you have no design on her before I
commit myself wholeheartedly to wooing her."

Nigel was furious. What right did this pompous ass have
to come in here and declare his intentions? He was about to
voice his grievance when Marcus' laughter rang throughout
the stable.

"At least that's settled." Nigel's mouth hung open. He was
about to speak when Marcus added, "It is clear as day that
you love her."

NIGEL'S MOUTH opened and closed, but no words were
forthcoming. He stood speechless for several more seconds.
Marcus waited for the denial, quite amused by Nigel's reaction to his disclosure. He could not recall a time when his
friend had kept silent for so long.

A small part of Marcus envied the love he saw between
Nigel and Artemisia. But he knew all too well what evils
lurked when a man let his guard down. *He* would never let
one woman affect him so. He would never let his heart be
broken the way his father's had. He would never fall to his
knees, begging a woman for anything.

When at last Nigel formed words, they were rough, grav-
elly. "Then you should stay away from her." He sank his
pitchfork into another bale.

Marcus knew Nigel, and his rakish ways, too well to
allow him to hurt Artemisia. His tone turned grave. "She is

like a sister to me." He squared his shoulders, his facial muscles tensing with restraint. "If you hurt her, I will kill you."

"Is that a threat?" Nigel raised a brow.

"Just a warning." Marcus' tone was light, but his sentiment was deadly.

Walking away from Nigel, Marcus was pleased that he'd ruffled his friend's feathers. He had meant what he said. He *would* kill Nigel if he caused Artemisia any grief.

CHAPTER 15

*T*he hour was early, the morning sun still hours from making its presence known. Servants would not be about the house yet. Artemisia paced back and forth across the rich Aubusson rug. She wanted to confess all to Nigel. After all, he had been honest with her about his part in sabotaging her wedding. But her secret was nothing like that. After the humiliation had begun to fade, she'd found she was most pleased about not having to marry Mr. Chartwick.

She wasn't sure Nigel would be as pleased when he discovered that she not only helped plan Philippa's elopement, but also knew her sister's current whereabouts. She did not want to cause discord within the Monfort household, but loyalty to her own family always came first.

Then she had a sobering thought. What if by not telling Nigel, she was sacrificing *her* chance at happiness? Although he had never discussed marriage with her, she assumed that after his confessions, and especially after they'd made love, he would *want* to marry. But it was easier to list the why nots than count the reasons why he would propose.

She started to think of all the reasons why someone like

Nigel would not marry someone like her. It was the same list as always; too dark, too tall, can't dance, too curvaceous…

No. I can dance now, and I do have a nice singing voice, and who cares if I am too tall, Nigel is much taller than I am. And watching him pleasure her had been all too seductive. She no longer feared her body. All the reasons why she'd deemed herself not suitable over the years were now erased by the way Nigel had made love to her.

Despite the early hour, or the fact that Nigel might not even be awake, she decided she was going to confess her involvement in her sister's elopement.

With her mind made up, she walked across the hall and knocked softly on his bedroom door before she lost her nerve.

The moment Nigel opened it, her world burst into a thousand twinkling stars. Her body tingled at the sight of his tanned muscular chest as he stood in front of her wearing nothing but buff-colored breeches.

"I was hoping that you would visit me," he said, pulling her into his room and kissing her fervently until she felt lightheaded.

Upon hearing the door close, she muttered between kisses, "What… are you… doing?"

Biting her ear, he growled, "I am making you want me as much as I want you."

"It… it's working." All rational thought flew out of her mind. She could barely remember why she'd knocked on his door wearing nothing more than her night rail and dressing gown.

Nigel untied the robe and tossed it to one side. Within a matter of seconds, she was standing in front of him, completely naked. Strong, roaming hands slid down the side of her torso. "I adore your body."

For the first time in her life, her curves, ample bosom, and height did not bother her. Backing her up against the wall, he kissed his way down her chest, going down on his knees in front of her.

With a wicked gleam in his eyes, he held her in place with one hand, while the other grabbed her leg and guided it up over his shoulder.

He smiled up at her, then plunged his tongue into her soft folds. Lifting his head for only a moment, he enticed, "Watch me pleasure you."

She had never seen anything so erotic as the sight of his head between her legs. Her own head fell back against the wall with a soft thump. Her knees wobbled. She thought she might faint on the spot.

Two strong hands gripped her thighs, holding her upright. Despite the pressure from where his fingers dug into her skin, she felt safe with him. She bucked against him as passion consumed her, and then slid down the wall an inch. He caught her in his arms and carried her to the bed.

No sooner had he laid her down than he divested himself of his remaining clothes and joined her. He hovered mere inches above her. Her hands ached to explore. She took her time traversing across his broad, firm chest, feeling his heart pound against one of her hands as the other travelled down towards his manhood. Her body demanded more. She wanted him to thrust inside her, drive himself deep into her core. "Please Nigel," she whispered against his mouth as she touched him.

She saw stars when his finger began to swirl about her sex. "You are so wet for me." He licked his way up her neck. "I want to do this all day and all night."

"What if my aunt needs me?"

"She has servants to tend to her needs." He sucked one

nipple until it puckered beneath his ministrations. "*I* am tending to your many, many needs."

THE VIEW of the sloping meadow from the comfortable chair in the library was most impressive. Tall blades of green grass swayed in the breeze. In the far distance, a hawk swooped down, disappearing into the grass.

Resting his head against his intertwined fingers at the nape of his neck, Nigel stretched out his legs, contentment washing over him. The morning had been most productive. He'd made love to Artemisia twice before she'd snuck back to her room. He inhaled deeply and let out a slow, relaxed breath. Nothing could spoil his mood.

"Excuse me, Mr. Rochefort, this has just arrived for you."

Nigel had not noticed Simms entering the room. Standing up, he took the letter from the tray. Recognizing his mother's handwriting, he tore open the envelope, worried that some ill had befallen their family.

The letter *was* cause for concern, but not what he'd first anticipated. His mother was most distraught over the news that was now circulating around London. The body of a young woman had been found washed up on the shore of the Thames, her features similar to those of Philippa Germayne. Although the body in question had not been identified as Phillipa's remains, the gossipmongers had concocted their own story, which placed all guilt on Nigel's doorstep. An official investigation was to take place post haste.

A vein in his neck pulsated. He was furious. The person responsible for this nightmare would pay.

Throwing the letter into the unlit fireplace, he growled out, "Damn it."

"What's the matter?"

Startled by the question, he turned around just as Artemisia strolled up to him. What would he tell her?

She looked too beautiful, almost angelic, wearing all white with her hair pulled back into a tidy chignon. He wanted to forget what he'd just read, and instead undo her hair and watch its lengthy tresses fall about her curvaceous form. *Damn*. Why did lustful thoughts always invade his mind in her presence? Clearing his throat, he responded. "Just tittle-tattle from London."

"You should not pay any attention to those hurtful women. They are just bitter and unhappy."

"Under normal circumstances, I would agree. But in this case, it affects my mother… and you." He saw the look of concern on Artemisia's face. He did not want to upset her with the rumors that surrounded her sister, but she would find out sooner or later. He wanted to be the one to console her. "It appears that the *ton* has decided that I am responsible for your sister's disappearance."

Confusion sounded in her voice. "Marcus had already conveyed as much when he arrived. I do not believe you were responsible. You simply offered advice."

Her faith in him touched his heart. "There has been a new development." He stepped in closer to her, bracing himself for tears and hysterics. "The body of a young woman was found beside the Thames. It is rumored to be that of your sister's."

Artemisia's eyes opened wide in shock. He thought she would cry or exhibit some other feminine emotion. In the past, he would have dreaded such outbursts, but his affection for her had grown such that he wanted to be a part of her life, to share joys and comfort her in times of need.

"Thank you for delivering that news. Please excuse me."

She turned and walked out of the room without so much as a single tear.

He blinked several times, then shook his head, wondering what had just happened.

He should have followed her, but he was too stunned to do anything but stand there, paralyzed. He must have dreamt the entire scene. Artemisia had not cried, or yelled and screamed, or even thrown a tantrum before she'd walked out of the room.

"What the bloody hell just happened?" he whispered into the silent room.

HIDING IN HER BEDROOM, Artemisia had managed to avoid Nigel for the rest of the day. Whenever he came to her door, Maggie was there to shoo him away. She sent word to her aunt that she was ill and would take her meal in her room. She was thankful that Aunt Lou did not question her actions.

She sat in her favorite chair, brushing her long locks. Her stomach was cramping, and her head throbbed as guilt ate away at her. The concerned look on Nigel's face when he'd delivered the news he'd thought might explain her sister's fate tore at her heart. She'd wanted to confess everything right then and there, but had been too stunned, or just too afraid, to admit her guilt.

Tomorrow. Tomorrow, she would confess everything.

Philippa would be hurt and disappointed when she discovered Artemisia had revealed her secret, but she hoped Philippa would forgive her and be happy that she, too, had found *the one*. It was a chance she was willing to take in order to spend the rest of her life with the only man that she ever had, or ever would, love.

CHAPTER 16

*A*rtemisia was surprised when she was informed that she had a visitor in the Green Parlor. She was half expecting—secretly hoping—to find Philippa there. All her troubles would be at an end if her sister were present. But when she entered the parlor, her step faltered at the sight of Weston. Without a doubt, she knew the investigator had discovered her involvement in her sister's elopement.

"I thought I would come to see you first before returning to London. Your father expects a full report. I suspect nothing I am about to tell you will come as a surprise." His voice was not accusatory, just matter-of-fact.

Shaking her head, Artemisia simply replied, "No, I don't suppose it will."

Perhaps she should confess her sins before Weston gave his report. She could not bear the thought that he might think ill of her. He was a trusted friend, and had been a frequent visitor to Knollwood when he and Marcus were at school together. The bastard son of a baron was not always welcomed in some circles, but Aunt Lou had never excluded those born on the wrong side of the blanket.

"Before you begin," she started on a long exhale, "I…I want to… explain why we concocted the story."

Weston's tone held none of the disdain she thought she deserved. "You don't have to do this, Artemisia."

"Yes, I do." She strolled to the window. The sky was grey, threatening the land with rain. It was a miserable day that matched her mood. "When Mr. Keates proposed to Philippa, she was so happy, so in love. She knew our father would disapprove of the match. I was about to be married—so certain that my future would be a happy one." She turned around to face Weston. "I wanted her to be happy, too. Philippa would never be content to marry someone because he came from a good family or had a title. She declared when she was but a little girl that she would only marry for love."

"She made that announcement to a crowded church when a distant cousin married a man old enough to be her grandfather, if I remember correctly." He chuckled at that recollection.

"Yes, she was always one for dramatics." Circling her foot on the elegant rug, Artemisia took a deep breath and continued, "When Philippa asked me to aid in her elopement with Mr. Keates, I could not deny her. I never could." And that had always been one of her biggest problems, Artemisia acknowledged. She had always been so enthralled by her beautiful younger sister that she'd put her own best interests aside so that Philippa could have her heart's desire.

"I understand."

"Do you?" Artemisia questioned in disbelief. "How can you comprehend the situation when I am only beginning to understand myself?"

"I feel much the same about my little sister." Weston approached her by the window. "Why did you not squash the rumors concerning your sister and Mr. Rochefort? You could have easily done so without raising an alarm about Philippa's true plans."

The conversation had turned most uncomfortable. Looking back, she should have gone to Weston the moment that Philippa had concocted her scheme. But she hadn't. And now, the guilt and secrets were tearing her apart. She had to confide in someone. "Nigel..." She released a long, hard sigh. "He hurt me years ago, and I wanted to make him pay for those cruel words."

"And has he?"

"I'm afraid that I am the one who will suffer in the end." She would confess everything to Nigel, and prayed that he would forgive her.

NIGEL WAS ABOUT to leave for the stables when he heard Simms announce the arrival of Weston. He was familiar with the man, having often spent holidays at Knollwood with him and Marcus. He also knew of his work as an investigator and wondered if he brought further news regarding Philippa. When he approached the Green Parlor, he noticed the door was closed and Simms stood guard. Something odd was going on.

He crept outside and went around to the side of the house. Shoving an outstretched branch of a shrub aside, he scrambled around for the latch that opened the door leading into the secret passageway.

It only took a matter of moments to reach the end of the dark hall. Pressing his ear to the door, he heard Artemisia's muted voice. *"When Mr. Keates proposed to Philippa."* So, Philippa was not in harm's way. No ill had befallen her. It was all a lie!

He pressed even harder up against the door, not wanting to miss a single word. *"Nigel… he hurt me years ago, and I wanted to make him pay for those cruel words."*

Was this some kind of savage game? His anger was at a boiling point. Even after he'd confessed his wrongdoings, she continued with this charade. What of his mother? She knew how his mama suffered because of the rumors, and yet Artemisia could only think of making him pay for words that he already apologized for. Well, two could play at that game. He turned away from the door, too disgusted to listen further.

AFTER ADMITTING her involvement in Philippa's elopement to Weston, Artemisia knew it was imperative she confessed to Nigel, too. She was determined to set everything to right. She looked all over the house for him, but when he was nowhere to be found, she searched all their favorite haunts outside— the oak courtyard, the rose garden. Half an hour later, she still had not located him. In this weather, she did not think he would go for a ride, but the stable was the only place left where he could be.

The scent of damp earth lingered in the air, the dark sky threatening to unleash its anger once again at any moment. She picked up her pace, walking as fast as she could towards the stables.

He was almost finished with saddling Orazio, so she rushed to his side. "I wanted to tell…" Her voice sounded feeble, even to her own ears.

His face was red with anger. His voice was harsh, almost cruel. "Save your lies, Miss Germayne."

Miss Germayne? He knew. "Let me explain."

He turned his back on her. "No. I don't want to hear

excuses. You lied to me. Even after we made love, you continued to lie to me."

"I only did it to protect my sister. She made me promise to keep her secret and not to say anything." Her voice was full of anger and emotion. She yelled at the top of her lungs, "Surely *you* can understand family loyalty."

"What is that supposed to mean?"

She did not know what to say to make him believe her. "If the situation were reversed, what would you have done?"

"You did not trust me." She heard the hurt in his words. He tightened a strap on Orazio's bridle, and the animal protested the rough movement.

Nigel had his faults, but honesty and loyalty were of the uppermost importance to him. She knew this, and yet she'd chosen to continue to lie to him.

"I could not betray her trust. If anyone should understand that, it is you."

Nigel faced her, and her heart missed a beat. For one brief moment, her hopes rose before they were shattered into a thousand pieces by the unforgiving look that overtook his features.

Her body trembled with the fear of losing him. "Please say you understand," she cried.

He shook his head, turned away, and finished tacking up Orazio, then led the large brown horse past Artemisia, out into the yard. "No, I don't understand. Instead of confiding in me, you'd have me suffer, would have my mother suffer as rumors swirled throughout London that I was a debaucher of young women and a murderer. You said you cared for me." His gaze was deadened by the anguish that *she* had caused him. "But obviously not enough to trust me."

She'd never meant to deceive him. She'd only wanted to

protect her sister. She stepped closer to him. "Nigel, if you could grant me time to explain."

Her words fell on deaf ears.

He mounted his horse with one swift movement. He did not even look her way when he bid farewell. "Goodbye, Miss Germayne."

She stood and watched him gallop off into the distance. "I cannot believe he left," she murmured into the wind. He would not even hear her explanation. As if his leaving was not bad enough, he'd left in anger. No, anger was too mild a word. Furious. He'd been furious with her about her deception.

Damn him, I should be angrier with him, not the other way around!

What of his actions and deceit? Were they any less than hers? Family loyalty was important to both of them. He would have done the same if the situation were reversed. *Only he confessed and made amends. You did not.*

Her conscience was draining her soul and getting the better of her.

Why would she reveal her sister's secret? She did not want Lady Monfort to suffer, but had to think of her sister. Over the last week, she had convinced herself that Nigel's mother had grown used to the scandal and gossip that always surrounded her son. It was just another *on dits*, nothing more. Except it wasn't *nothing more*, not when it destroyed their chance at happiness.

She walked back towards the house. She wanted to find a way to get Nigel to listen to her, to understand why she was so determined to protect her sister. She contemplated her destination. She did not want to sit in her room and sulk. Whenever she was upset, she went to the Great Oak for comfort. Despite the weather being cold and damp, she did not care. However, she did not believe that even her favorite spot could raise her downtrodden spirits. But it was worth a try.

A shiver rippled down her spine as she entered the courtyard. Rubbing her arms, she strolled beneath the Great Oak, contemplating all that had happened.

The moment Nigel had discovered the truth, he'd left her. What would she do? She was ruined. Not that she'd had any prospects before coming to Knollwood. But somehow this felt worse.

"Aunt Louella told me I would find you here."

She tried to hide her feelings that were knotting her insides. "What do you want, Marcus?"

"I want to make things right." The sincerity in his voice made her heart ache even more.

"And how do you intend to do that? You were not the one to leave." She sniffed back a sob. She would not cry. Nigel did not deserve her tears.

Marcus sat down on the root beside her. He raised her chin with a single finger and turned her head towards him. "Marry me. You can be mistress of Knollwood. We get on well together, and there have been far worse matches in history."

The offer was tempting, too tempting. She had always loved Knollwood. If he had asked her a week ago, she would have jumped at the opportunity, but so much had changed. Marcus was just trying to protect her, and she loved him—as a brother—all the more for that. But she was in love with another man… *who doesn't want you.*

What if she was carrying his child? *Oh no*, she hadn't even thought of that very real possibility.

"I don't know," she shook her head, wishing she had a better answer. "It's just that I…"

"You love him." It was not a question, but a statement. "Artemisia," Marcus started, taking her hand in his, "I know you do not love me in that way, and I love you only as a brother could." He paused, closing his eyes, and shaking his head. "With all honesty, I do not think I am capable of the all-consuming love that the legend of this oak portends."

She followed his gaze up through the scrollwork of branches as if searching for answers.

Lowering his gaze back to hers, he declared, "But I do know that we suit each other. I know you will make a wonderful marchioness and mother. If Nigel does not come around… all I ask is that you think about it."

She nodded her head in acquiescence. His proposal was most genuine, and his offer touched her heart.

When Simms informed her that Mr. Chartwick had arrived and wanted to speak with her, she thought it was some cruel prank. She was not up to this visit. First Nigel, then Marcus, and now the man who'd started all her current woes. It was too much to bear in one day. All she wanted was to escape to her room and cry.

But when she walked into the Pink Parlor, there was Mr. Chartwick in the flesh, sitting on a green damask settee. He appeared even more nervous than she, if that were possible, as he jumped to his feet.

Chartwick's voice cracked. "I want to apologize for…" He ran a single finger around the inside of his cravat, as if the material was strangling him. Clearing his throat, he continued, "for… what I did on our…"

She felt sorry for him as she lowered herself into a chair. She knew she shouldn't, but she did. "It is of no consequence now." And it wasn't. She was in love with Nigel, and nothing else mattered. Well, nothing except winning the heart of the man she'd betrayed. Looking at Chartwick now, sitting nervously across from her, she wondered what she'd ever seen in him.

Mr. Chartwick was a head shorter than Nigel, with brown hair, and even darker brown eyes. He sat with his neck slumped into his shoulders, while his fingers fumbled with edges of his riding coat. He appeared more like a feeble mouse with a piece of cheese than a full-grown man of eight and twenty.

"I did not mean to hurt you. I just… I mean… I was in love with someone else."

"Although I regret I did not learn earlier that your feelings were engaged elsewhere, I harbor no ill will against you or…"

"Annabelle Duncane."

She smiled at him, trying to ease his nerves. "Yes, Miss Duncane. I wish you both much happiness."

"Thank you, Miss Germayne, you are far too kind. If there is anything I can do to return the favor, please ask."

She thought for a moment, her mind racing with possibilities. Perhaps she could use Chartwick's visit to her advantage. "There is something that you can do for me."

Chartwick shifted in his seat with uneasiness. Although she sensed his words were sincere, he apparently had not anticipated that she would actually ask him for assistance.

"What was Mr. Rochefort's role in your decision?" She wanted to know if Nigel had been telling her the truth, that it was, in fact, all his doing.

Chartwick looked down at his interlocked hands, then raised them to his forehead, and shook his head. "I confided in him. Told him that I did not love you the way a fiancé should, that I was in love with someone else. That I only ever loved Annabelle. He told me that it was unfair, that I should give up the woman I love because of social restrictions."

He looked like someone who had just been socked in the stomach. His face contorted in pain. And then Artemisia realized it was not actually pain but distress. He began sobbing. She had never seen such an embarrassing display from a man. It was most disturbing. *Thank heavens I did not marry this sop!*

Without looking at her, he continued to speak through heavy gulps. "I should have just told you, but it was easier to take Nigel's offer and disappear with Annabelle."

Her ears perked up. "Nigel's offer?"

"He offered to pay off my father's debt so that Annabelle and I could marry." Sniffling back his tears, Chartwick continued, "He said that if we were truly in love, then we deserved to be together, despite all the obstacles."

Artemisia was numb. The lump in her throat became more painful with the realization of what Nigel meant to her, and what her own deception had done.

Chartwick must have thought the emotion displayed was for him, because he started blubbering like an absolute idiot. "Say you forgive me, please. I could not live with myself if I thought…"

"Mr. Chartwick, control yourself. I forgive you, but I must ask a favor."

Hiccupping on his sobs, he swore, "For your forgiveness, I will do anything you ask."

She needed to plan her course with great care if she were to win Nigel back. He did not trust her, and worse, he felt betrayed. She should be just as angry with him for his role in ruining her wedding day, but for the life of her, she could not. She knew now that Nigel had done what he'd done because he wanted her for himself.

Nigel's jealous streak had started the current predicament. Perhaps she could use that same jealous nature to her benefit.

However, she did not trust Mr. Chartwick not to reveal more than she intended. He had never been one to hold his tongue when information presented itself. With vagueness in mind, she requested, "I must ask that you make it known that we had a mutual agreement to not marry."

He gave her a confused look. "But how could we have had an agreement when I left you at the altar?"

"It was under the guise of another plan. You were in love with Annabelle, and I had my heart set on a notorious rake. My parents would have never agreed to such a match, so I had to take matters into my own hands and be seen as ruined in the eyes of the *ton*. You were able to elope with your love, and the rake came to my rescue." Artemisia paused for dramatic effect. "I hope to be married very soon as well."

"Oh, excuse me, Arte," Marcus entered the room, looking more handsome than ever. His timing could not have been more perfect. "My aunt wanted me to inform you that she will not join us this evening."

"Thank you, Marcus."

Marcus strolled up to Chartwick, his eyes cold, his jaw firm. Chartwick cowered under his scrutiny. Artemisia wanted to laugh. She hoped Marcus would keep up the pretense of the angered relative, but not take it too far. She wanted to scare Chartwick, not have him die of fright.

She decided to rescue Chartwick from his torture. "I believe we are finished here. I wish you a pleasant journey back to London." And with that, she stood and took Marcus' arm, leaving a terrified and bewildered Chartwick in the Pink Parlor.

Several feet down the hall, Marcus leaned in and whispered, "What was all that about?"

"I am setting a trap for Nigel."

A robust laugh left his lips. "Better him than me."

CHAPTER 17

*A*rtemisia had lied to him. After all they had shared, she could not trust him with her secret. And scandal had grown from that secret and was destroying his mother. A small part of Nigel reminded him that it wasn't Artemisia's secret, but Philippa's. But he brushed that truth aside. If she had lied to him about this, what else was she hiding, or willing to hide? What skeletons lurked in her wardrobe?

Of course, he did sabotage her wedding, had followed her to Knollwood, and seduced her. What was he supposed to do? Once he had come to terms with how he felt about her, he was not about to let the woman he loved escape him.

He did not know what to think anymore. He understood her desire to protect her family. He had that same desire, and therein laid the problem. He'd begun to think of Artemisia as part of *his* family, someone he could trust. Based on her actions, she had not felt the same. Damn, but all this made his head ache.

By the time he reached London, he was in a foul mood. Shortly after his arrival, the servants scurried in the other direction, knowing better than to disturb him. He was thankful that his mother was away for the evening. He did not want to have to answer her questions.

Locking himself in his father's study, he plopped down on the large leather chair behind the desk that had always been his father's throne. Not even Ranulph had had the nerve to sit in this seat since their father's passing over a year and a half ago.

The portrait of the late Lord Monfort hanging over the mantle mocked him. *At the first sign of conflict, you deserted her.*

"I will never be like you," Nigel yelled into the dark space.

You ruined her and then abandoned her.

He reached for the decanter of whisky, and not bothering with a glass, removed the stopper and took several large gulps. The warm liquid burned down his throat, settling in his empty stomach.

"I will be a faithful husband. I will be a doting father." After each declaration, he took another gulp, sealing his commitment. The anger that had been consuming him for so long poured out of his aching soul. "I will never humiliate my wife."

Throwing a glass against the wall, he screamed, "Why wasn't I good enough for you?"

He took another deep swig of the amber liquid, and for the first in a long time, he lost himself in its intoxicating strength. He put his head on the cool surface of the desk. *Why wasn't I good enough?* rang through his whisky-soaked brain over and over.

NIGEL'S HEAD WAS THROBBING. Struggling to open his eyes, his hand went to his temple. "Why is my head pounding?"

Lifting his head, he gazed about the room in a cloudy haze, before realizing the pounding sound was not in his head, but came from someone on the other side of the door. With unstable feet, he rose from the chair and stumbled his way across the cold room.

He laid his head against the door, and with an unsteady hand, unlocked it. A moment later, it flew open, knocking him on the head.

"What the…?" His curse died off when he saw his mother enter the room.

"Fergusson said you had locked yourself in the study and would not open the door."

Nigel remembered nothing. He walked back to the desk and slid into the chair.

Pulling up another chair, his mother sat down beside him. He caught a whiff of her sweet perfume. It reminded him of youthful days long gone. He had often spent hours in his mother's company, hoping that his father would arrive and shower him with affection. It was a bittersweet time in his life. He'd cherished his time with his mother, but was always longing for attention from his father.

Rubbing his aching temples, he questioned, "Why did Father detest me so?"

"He did not detest you!" The look on Mother's face revealed her shock and surprise at his question. Her next words stirred those same emotions. "He loved you just as much as Ranulph."

His retort was laced with sarcasm. "He had an odd way of showing it." Nigel could never recall a warm embrace or kind word from his father when he was a child. He'd always been pushed aside. Papa had claimed that he was too busy with estate business to be bothered.

His mother sighed—a deep, sad sigh. "Perhaps I have done you a disservice."

"What is that supposed to mean?"

"Your father *did* love you, but he was afraid of losing you."

Nigel doubted that statement.

"And now it is too late." He heard the grief in his mother's voice.

What she'd said confused him. If his father had been so afraid of losing him, why had he continued to act like he hated the sight of him? Nigel wanted to ask the questions that had plagued his mind for so long, but did not know how far to push to get the answers he desired. The wound of losing her beloved husband was still too fresh for her to deal with the other realities of life at times. He sat and waited, hoping she would continue without prompting.

"After you were born, your father was so overjoyed." Her eyes brightened with her recollection. "He thought life was perfect. He had two fine sons, the estate was doing well, we were happy." Her expression changed, the frown on her face deepening. "And then, you took ill."

Nigel had only been an infant when he'd become unwell, too young to remember, but he'd heard the story often enough when growing up. The doctor had not known what caused the fever, or why he was so small, not gaining weight, or unable to keep milk down. He'd wavered on the verge of death for a year before he'd improved. Another two years had passed before he'd been deemed to be in satisfactory health. And still several more before his size had caught up to his age.

"He worried over you, wondering if you would live or die. There was one day in particular when your health took a turn for the worse. We were convinced that you would not survive the night." She closed her eyes as if reliving the painful memory. "Your father left the room in tears. After that horrible night, he never came to visit you again for fear that he would walk into the room and see you lying dead in your crib."

"But then I improved. Why did he not...?"

Shaking her head, she answered his unspoken question. "You did not improve right away. He was frightened of getting close to you, and then losing you. He had lost two brothers in infancy to similar symptoms. He'd seen his own mother and father suffer through their grief. In the end, your grandfather pushed all those he cared about aside. Your grandmother spoke to me only once on the subject, hoping that her son would not make the same mistake."

"It appears that he did."

"No, not right away. But once you had fully recovered, he was still convinced that the mysterious malady would return, and you would be taken from him. He may have appeared to be strong minded and void of emotions, but he was weak."

"Why did you not tell me this sooner?" Nigel thought of all those wasted years believing his father did not care for him.

"It was not that simple." There was a long pause, followed by a deep sigh. "Your father did not realize the distance he created, nor did I at first. You have to understand, we were married for quite a few years before I conceived Ranulph. We both thought that children were not to be part of our future. After Ranulph was born, your father became a different person. He was so caring and attentive. And then you were born, and our world was complete."

"But I ruined that." Nigel heard the bitterness in his own voice. It did not sit well with him.

His mother's eyes opened wide. Reaching for his hand, she exclaimed, "You did no such thing. What happened was out of our control."

"Why did he change? If he was happy before, then why did he not find joy in my recovery?"

She shook her head, as if trying to comprehend herself. "There were many factors that led to his change of personality."

"You mean Carlotta?" The moment Nigel spoke his father's mistress' name, he regretted it. The knowledge that his father had not remained faithful, and worse, had not hidden the fact, still caused his mother much heartache.

"Yes." Her heavy sigh nearly broke his heart. "What I am about to reveal is only to help you understand, not to place blame." She looked at him with such intensity, it almost frightened him. "Instead of coming to my bed and risk having another child who might be ill, he took a mistress. He did not want to cause me distress. He stayed away often and never spoke of what happened."

It was all coming back to him. Nigel remembered the night when his mother had found out about Carlotta. He'd been no more than six, and so excited to see his father. He'd waited up for him to return home from London. He could remember running up to Father in excitement, only to be brushed aside and told to go to bed.

Instead of obeying, he'd listened to his parents argue on the other side of the door to his father's study. It had been his first act of rebellion. His father had shouted at Mother when she'd asked why he'd been delayed. Nigel had felt frightened for her. Father's temper was always rather short, but even more so on that night.

"Why do you insist on plaguing me with questions? Do

you not see that I am protecting you? I don't want to hurt you!" Lord Monfort's voice had rumbled through the door.

Nigel did not hear his mother's quiet response, but by his reaction, knew she must have said something that displeased his father even more.

"Damn it! Just stop with the inquisition. This is why I seek comfort in London. Carlotta does not question me. Carlotta does not demand that I spend time with her. Carlotta—"

"Damn your Carlotta." It was the only time he ever recalled his mother shouting, or using blasphemy, for that matter.

Nigel remembered being scared and not wanting to hear anymore yelling or cruel words. He'd run as fast as his little legs would carry him, straight to his room, and dived under the bedcovers. Not long after, his mother had tiptoed in. He had not wanted her to know that he'd been listening, or how upset he was, so he'd pretended to be sleeping.

When his mother had sat on the bed, she'd caressed his hair with gentle strokes, easing the pain of his father's rejection. Whether she'd known he was asleep or not, he'd never found out. But something had happened that night so long ago. A bond had formed between him and his mother that his father resented. It all made sense now, but to a small child, he'd felt as if part of his world had just died.

She squeezed his hand, bringing him back into the present. "You have been one of my greatest joys."

"But don't you ever wonder if I had not been born…"

"No." Her answer came quick and was full of love. "If it wasn't your health, it would have been something else. Your father's expectations were often unreasonable. The only regret that I have is that it came at your expense."

Nigel reached out and pulled his mother into an embrace. "I don't want to be like him," he whispered into her ear.

"Then, go to her."

Pulling back, he looked at his dearest mama.

"Ever since the two of you first played together, I knew. Despite how much you would complain that Artemisia always wanted to tag along, or annoy you, you were never happier than after you'd seen her." She patted his cheek with affection. "Go to her."

It wasn't that simple. If his mother only knew what he had done.

CHAPTER 18

*A*rtemisia watched the familiar scenery of London pass by. So much had changed for her since the last time she was here. In the past few weeks, she had learned so much about who she was and what she wanted. No longer was she insecure about her looks and accomplishments. She suspected the coming days would be most trying, but she was up for the challenge and would not let the gossips—or anyone else—distract her. Now all she had to do was convince her parents.

Germayne House came into view, and in the short distance beyond, Monfort House. Would Nigel be in residence? Should she send a note? Her heart lurched with pain over her loss.

No. Marcus had advised her not to. She was not to act like a lovesick schoolgirl, desperate for attention. He knew Nigel best in that regard. Although she'd come up with a scheme, Marcus would be a crucial advisor in the success of the stratagem. He had arranged for a series of outings in which they would be seen together by the gossips. Once word made its rounds, Marcus believed it would not take long for Nigel to make an appearance.

The carriage came to a gentle halt in front of Germayne House. The door was bathed in a stream of golden sunlight. Descending the steps of the carriage, she shielded her eyes against the glare. Home. It did not feel like home anymore. She suspected that no place would, without Nigel. Artemisia steadied her nerves for the onslaught of questions that were sure to come from her parents once inside.

The front door flew wide open, followed by a flurry of silk and excitement. "You're finally here!" Philippa ran down the front path, shouting with delight.

Artemisia stood motionless, too shocked to move at the sight of her sister.

"Oh, how I have missed you," Philippa squealed while embracing her.

She pulled back and looked into her sister's blue eyes. All she saw was happiness. Lowering her voice, she inquired, "Have you not told Father about Mr. Keates?"

Philippa hugged her, and then, keeping one arm about Artemisia's waist, led her back towards the house. "I was so nervous when we arrived. But Father listened most attentively and welcomed Mr. Keates. He is not pleased with what we did, but he is relieved that no harm came to me." She leaned in closer and lowered her voice. "I suspect after the rumors that have been circulating, Father would not have minded if I'd married a monkey just as long as I came home."

Artemisia giggled at the thought of Philippa walking down the aisle with a monkey for a groom. "I am so happy for you both." And she was. But her sister's happiness had come at a heavy price for her.

"But what of you, dear sister? Mother has not spoken two words about what happened with your Mr. Chartwick."

Artemisia was saved from having to answer by her mother's squeals of delight. "Oh, two of my girls are home."

Only neither of them was a girl anymore. Artemisia just smiled and let her mother relish her joy. She did not want to spoil the moment with talk of her current woes.

Glancing about, her mother inquired, "I thought Louella was joining you?"

"Aunt Lou decided to follow in a couple of days in her own carriage."

Thankfully, no further explanation was needed, and her mother guided her and Philippa into the house as if nothing untoward had taken place.

A short time later, Artemisia sat quite still beside her mother, waiting for her father to start shouting. Instead, he joined them on the large settee. When he turned to face her, she could see the hurt in his eyes. Bile rose in her throat. What had she done? Would her parents ever forgive her?

"Why did you not come to us?" His voice held no hint of anger or disappointment, only love and concern.

She let out a long sigh before answering. "I promised her. She thought you would never approve of Mr. Keates."

It just did not seem fair. Philippa had found true love, eloped to Gretna Green, and was welcomed—with her new husband, whose station was far beneath hers—back into the bosom of her family, all with no consequences.

Even the rumors surrounding her sister's scandalous elopement had been pushed aside in favor of more intriguing gossip: Artemisia.

Philippa was enjoying her new life as a married woman, while Artemisia sat here beside her parents, feeling guilty for what she had done to them and to Nigel.

Steeling her nerves, she gritted her teeth, waiting for the

lecture. However, much to her surprise, it wasn't forthcoming.

"Your father and I have decided to reintroduce you into society. Marcus has agreed to accompany you to various upcoming events. Please understand that we are in no hurry to marry you off and will let you decide when the time comes, but for now, we do not want to see you pining away."

Artemisia should have felt as if she'd been handed the world. After all, this was the outcome she had hoped for after Chartwick abandoned her at the altar.

"I don't know what to say." Her mind was reeling with all that had occurred over the last week.

Her father's gentle voice broke through the haze. "Don't say anything. We are Germayne's and we will rise above petty gossip. And you *will* find love."

Little did her father realize that she already had found it. Found and already lost it.

ARTEMISIA WAS uncomfortable with all the attention she was receiving. Previously, she had been overlooked at balls because of her poor dancing skills and untraditional appearance. But now, every young gent wanted to make her acquaintance. She did not understand why, given the turn of events.

Of course, her popularity was bittersweet. She used to dream of being the belle of the ball, and having handsome young men fawn all over her. But now the one man she wanted was nowhere to be seen.

Miss Walker's engagement ball had to be the dullest affair that she ever had attended. Her boredom only added to her melancholy. She had not seen Nigel since his hasty departure from Knollwood. She did not even know if he had returned to London. How was her scheme to be successful if Nigel wasn't even in Town? How could she have misjudged Nigel? How could he have misjudged her intentions so? She was certain that if he would just listen to reason, they could make amends.

Upon her reintroduction to society, she'd tried to squash any rumors. If asked about Mr. Chartwick, she answered with a vague, "It was a mutual decision not to marry." Although everyone knew it was not. She had been humiliated in the chapel all those weeks ago for a number of reasons.

She stared across the ballroom, hardly noticing those around her. She did not want to be here. Town had lost what little luster it held for her.

Her mother joined her. "Why don't you hint to Marcus to ask you to dance?"

It was rather ironic. Now that she had the confidence to dance without trampling on her partner's toes, she had no desire to.

"I am not feeling up to dancing quite yet, Mother." Since her return from Knollwood, her mother had become most concerned with her well-being. Artemisia appreciated the concern of her family, but she needed time to heal. She could not very well tell them what Nigel had done, what they had shared, and how she longed to be in his arms once again.

The room had become rather stuffy. She needed to escape all the gossiping and stares, and strolled out onto the dim veranda.

"Do you mind if I join you?" a masculine voice asked from behind.

She turned at the sound of Marcus' voice. "That would be most pleasant, Marcus."

"Well, I don't know about that. My mood is foul this

evening," he said with a hint of laughter. "It appears I am fair game for the mamas."

Artemisia knew his quip was an attempt to improve her spirits. Although it didn't help, she appreciated the effort.

"Then we are perfect company." She tried to sound sincere.

Marcus walked beside her. If she did not think of him as a brother, she would have thought him the most handsome man in Town. His eyes sparkled with the same mischievousness as Nigel's.

Nigel.

"Thinking about the scoundrel again?"

"Is it that obvious?" Why did she continue to think about that rogue?

Putting his arm around her waist, Marcus brought her into his embrace. Artemisia rested her head on his chest. His voice resonated deep within. "Oh, my little sprite, it is."

She buried her head and cried.

Tongues were wagging by the time they reentered the ballroom. "I will not let you leave," Marcus whispered into her ear. "Let's give the old biddies something to gossip about." Giving her no choice but to follow, he led her onto the dance floor.

The gossipmongers had been itching all evening to leave and spread their tales. Marcus' unwillingness to part with Artemisia only added fuel to the fire, and by the end of the evening, she and he had given them enough gossip to last for days.

CHAPTER 19

$\mathcal{N}$igel was late. He had hesitated about coming, but his desire to see Artemisia was greater than anything he had ever experienced. Their feud had gone on long enough. He went through the entrance hall, heading straight for the ballroom.

Moving through the crowded room, he heard his name murmured by several tongues. He did not care. He was here for one reason alone: Artemisia. There was still no sign of her by the time he had walked the length of the room.

Standing by the open veranda door, he started to stretch his neck to see if he could spot her through the crush. He was about to give up and take his leave when he heard the voice of his ex-best friend. "Oh, my little sprite, it is."

Glancing out on to the veranda, he saw Artemisia and Marcus in a passionate embrace. Adrenaline rushed through his body. If it were not for the tittle-tattle that would destroy his mother, he would have confronted the bastard right then and there. His blood was pounding in his ears. He had to get away before he did something he truly regretted. Turning around, he stormed out of the room. Let the rumors fly.

He could not get the image of Artemisia and Marcus out of his mind. Marcus had had his arm around her waist, with Artemisia—*his* Artemisia—leaning into him. Marcus' words had been soft and caring. Not full of hate and anger, as Nigel's had been the last time he'd seen Artemisia. No wonder she'd gone to Marcus for comfort. *Damn him.*

After what he'd witnessed, and the little bit of conversation he'd overheard, he needed to think. No, perhaps not think, but drink. Not wanting to encounter his mother at home, he went straight to White's.

No sooner had he settled himself into a brown leather armchair, brandy in hand, than his plan to wallow in excessive drink was interrupted.

Chartwick plopped down in the chair beside him. "I did it. I am a free man."

"How can you be a free man when you are only recently married? I thought you would be feeling the chains of marriage stifling your every move, not liberating you."

"I made a clean slate of it, old boy. I went to see Artemisia, and she forgave me for what I did."

"Good for you." Nigel's words came out more harshly than he'd intended. His mood was dark and foreboding. He did not want to socialize but to drink himself into oblivion, and perhaps hit something. Chartwick might do. The man had no idea he was in danger of being pummeled.

Sitting back, Chartwick sighed, most pleased with himself. "Everything worked out. I am married to Annabelle, and Artemisia will soon be happily settled as well."

Nearly choking on his brandy, Nigel sat forward with a start. "What did you say?" He must have misheard.

"Artemisia is to marry Hawthorne."

"She told you that she was going to marry Marcus?" The hair on the back of Nigel's neck stood on end.

Betrayed by that ass!

"Not in so many words. But she talked of a rake and marriage, and then Marcus entered the room and whisked her away." Chartwick gulped the last of the contents in his glass, adding, "They do make a nice pair."

No, they did not make a nice pair. He was going to kill Marcus.

He and Artemisia made a nice pair. There was no possible way that he was going to let Marcus claim what was his. Without bidding Chartwick farewell, Nigel stood and pushed his way through White's. He did not care who saw, or for the comments that were sure to be whispered about his behavior. Let them talk. He was going to put an end to this… tonight.

He stepped out of White's. The night had turned cold and few were out on the streets. Even so, he worked up a sweat in his haste to reach Germayne House.

"I'm sorry, sir, but the family has gone out for the evening. Would you like to leave word?"

"No." His answer was short and curt. He walked down the steps, formulating another plan. She would not get off this easily.

Meandering to the back of the house, his plan firm in his mind. As he opened the garden gate, it squeaked, but fortunately, there was no sign of life to raise the alarm.

A light haze of fog had infiltrated the city a short time ago, providing the perfect cloak for mischievousness. He had just reached the servants' entrance when the side door opened. Ducking behind an obliging tree, he hoped that he had not been seen.

"I could lose my position if I am caught," a young woman's voice whispered into the night.

"I only want a kiss," a man responded. After which there was only silence. Nigel presumed the young woman had given into the request. Only Nigel knew better. It was never just one kiss.

Sliding out from behind the tree, he entered the house through the door the pair had left open. If they were trying to avoid detection, then the way must be clear. He paused while his eyes adjusted to the dark room.

The servants' stairs that led to the second floor were a better choice than marching into the entrance hall and up the grand staircase. He could not risk anyone being alerted to his presence.

The stairwell was dark but quiet. When he reached the landing, he opened a door a few inches. He heard movement at the far end of the hall, closed the door, and waited.

Patience was not his virtue. It felt like an eternity before the sound of maids' voices faded along the passageway. He did not know which room was Artemisia's, only that hers faced the garden. Which eliminated half the rooms on the floor.

The first room with a garden outlook that he came upon was dark and cold from disuse. He moved to the next. When he opened the door, the fresh scent of lavender filled his nostrils. His body instantly reacted, knowing without a doubt that this was her bedroom.

Moving inside, he closed the door behind him. A soft glow from the fireplace cast shadows about the elegant boudoir. He would wait for her to return.

MISS WALKER'S engagement ball had proceeded just as Artemisia and Marcus had hoped. Chartwick had not kept silent about her insinuation of marriage, and it was all the gossipmongers could talk about.

Throughout, Marcus was a most attentive pretend suitor. He showered her with compliments, fetched her punch, and kept the naysayers away. He was also the handsomest man in attendance. Every young lady had glared at her with envy. But she was too preoccupied watching new arrivals, because she hoped Nigel would somehow appear, to take full notice of those around her.

When they arrived home, Marcus bid Artemisia and her family farewell in the hall, before taking his leave. Her parents, sister and new brother-in-law retired to the library to play cards, but she had no desire to join them.

Artemisia knew it was only a matter of time before she saw Nigel again, but she was anxious, nonetheless. What would they say to each other? Would he finally forgive her?

Contemplating these questions, she ascended the stairs, pulling the pins from her hair in the process. By the time she reached the landing on the second floor, she had a handful of pins, and her hair fell about her waist. She looked forward to climbing into bed, hoping that sleep would not elude her again.

Turning the knob, she entered her room and closed the door, intending to ring for her maid. The next thing she knew, she had been turned around and pressed against the door. Before she even had time to scream, a firm, demanding mouth came down upon hers.

Consumed with relief, she knew the instant his lips met hers, it was Nigel.

Nigel.

He smelled of leather and soap, and he was here, with her. His tongue flicked over her lips, enticing her to open up to him further. She obliged and sank into the kiss. When his mouth left hers and travelled down her neck, she thought she would faint with pleasure. It had been too long.

"I will make you forget Marcus if it is the last thing I do," he whispered fiercely into her ear before gently biting her lobe.

"He is already forgotten."

Nigel pulled back. The look on his face was a mixture of anger and confusion and past betrayal.

She was never going to let him leave her again. "I never said I was going to marry Marcus."

"You told Chartwick that—"

Leaning in, she cut him off with a flick of her tongue on his lips, followed by a kiss. "I told Chartwick that a rake came to my rescue." She clasped her hands about his face and forced him to look at her. "Nigel, that rake was you. You rescued me and gave me hope that my dreams might come true."

"But he said that you would marry soon."

"I said that I hoped to be married in due course. And I do."

As the realization of what she had actually revealed dawned on him, his face lit with a brilliant smile. "I should be angry with you, but for the life of me, I cannot."

"I should be angry with you," she teased in return.

"Why?"

She began to go through her reasons; "You ruined my wedding. You created a scandal for my sister. Then, you followed me to the country and seduced me." She reached up and brushed a soft kiss across his cheek. "Thank you."

His response came not in words but in actions. He led her in a sensuous waltz across the room. With each twirl, another piece of clothing floated to the floor. By the time they reached the bed, they were both naked. The moment their bodies touched the covers, their love play became a frenzy of need and want.

"You are mine," he declared.

She giggled, "Yours?"

"Mine," he whispered against her ear before his mouth traced a path down to her breast. He took one nipple in his mouth and suckled.

She thought she would faint from sheer pleasure. "Nigel," she cried out, "please."

He ignored her pleas and suckled the other nipple. She arched her back, desperate to be closer to him.

Flipping her onto her stomach, he grasped her hips and raised her up onto her knees. The position seemed odd, but who was she to argue? Nigel was the rake, not her. She could not see what he was doing, but the moment she felt the tip of his manhood enter her wet sheath, she sighed with a moan of pure pleasure. One of his hands reached around her body to rub her sensitive nub, while the other cupped her breast.

"You're so tight," he growled out with a need that matched her own.

He pushed deeper and deeper into her body. The delicious pressure was building. "Oh, yes."

His hands gripped her hips as he drove himself hard into her, their mutual needs bringing them to new heights of passion. With one final thrust, he filled her with his seed.

COMPLETELY SATED, Nigel rolled to his side, taking Artemisia with him. This was where he wanted her—naked beside him, always.

She raised her head and looked into his eyes. Hers were filled with tears. "I am so sorry to have ever deceived you."

He kissed the tip of her nose. "I am sorry that I ruined your wedding, scandalized your sister, followed you to the country, and seduced you."

"Are you?"

"No." He kissed her to seal his commitment. He most certainly wasn't.

EPILOGUE

$\mathcal{N}$igel guided the horses down the lane that led to Kettleworth. With Artemisia at his side, all felt right with the world. He could not have asked for a more perfect day. The sky was a brilliant shade of blue and the air was fresh and cool, a light breeze carrying the scent of autumn. The leaves had begun to change color and vivid shades of yellow and red welcomed him and his new bride home.

Pulling the curricle to a halt at the crest of the great park, he welcomed her to his home with pride. "Your new abode, my lady."

Her eyes opened wide with delight. "It is breathtaking."

He loved her reaction to her new home and took his time approaching the house, pointing out his favorite haunts along the way. "Over yonder is the hedge maze, and just beyond, a classical pavilion."

He watched her take in all that was around them. Although she did not speak, her smile spoke volumes.

When at last they reached Kettleworth House, with its impressive Corinthian portico and wide sweeping stairs,

Nigel had never been happier or more content. The woman beside him was responsible for this overwhelming joy, which only grew with each breath he took.

Ignoring the staff, Nigel picked up his new bride and carried her over the threshold into his favorite place in the house.

Setting her down in the center of the Great Marble Hall, Nigel watched Artemisia's gaze travel up the alabaster columns, past the Corinthian capitals, coming to rest on the Vitruvian scroll frieze. He held his breath in anticipation.

"It is magnificent." She reached up and kissed his cheek. "I could not imagine a more perfect home."

Pride swelled in his heart. He'd been worried that she would not care for his home the way she cared for Knollwood. Her sweet kiss wiped away those doubts.

He pulled her into him and guided her into a waltz. "I want to take you to *my* bed and make love to you all day and all night without worrying that it is improper or that someone will walk in on us."

She leaned back in his embrace and smiled up at him. "We cannot stay in bed all the time."

"Why not?" He dared her, twirling her about and kissing her in the process. Heat rose between them, leaving no doubt in his mind that they *could* stay in bed all the time.

"I do not believe that I have properly thanked you for sabotaging my wedding."

"And how do you intend to do that?"

A provocative gleam entered her eyes. His little siren was a most enchanting seductress. "Take me to our room and let me show you what I have in mind."

It was the perfect beginning to their happily ever after.

Want to know what happens next? Keep reading for a chapter excerpt from
Mistletoe Waltz
Book Three in *A Waltz with Destiny* Series…

Chapter One from Mistletoe Waltz

DECEMBER 26, 1820, Boxing Day

"THANK YOU, my lady. Primrose is my favorite color!" Faith's lady's maid exclaimed with a combination of surprise and joy. "I've never had fabric this lovely before." The tears in Troth's eyes spoke volumes, and it warmed Faith's heart to see the effect her gifts had. Everyone at Deer Park had been so welcoming since her arrival four months previous. Not having had a lady in residence for twenty-five years, they were eager to please, and Faith wanted to show her appreciation for all they had done.

"And this is for you, Caspar. Thank you for your dedicated service." The look of disbelief when he opened his gift filled Faith with delight. Although this was a foreign world to her, it was just how she had imagined Boxing Day would be at all the grand estates. It had been such a joyous day for her and she could not keep the smile off her face.

"Lady Hawthorne, I don't know what to say." Caspar ran his hand across the small, dark brown leather book.

"You're most welcome, Caspar." As she turned to pick up another gift from the adorned table, her skirt brushed Balder's head. The dog looked up at her but did not raise his head from the ornate jonquil rug, his black wirehair coat a bold and direct contrast to the rug's vibrant colors.

Just then, a cool breeze whipped through the room, sending a shiver down her spine.

Pine and leather invaded her senses. Even before she turned toward the source, she knew her husband had returned to Deer Park.

Balder jumped to a sitting position, his ears perked up, a slight snarl rumbling past his jaws. Faith patted his head as much for his comfort as for hers.

A moment later, she heard the deep masculine voice of her husband growling at her. "What are you doing?"

Swallowing hard, she turned to face him. He stood larger and more handsome than she remembered, but his honey-colored eyes were not as soft and caring as they had been on the first night when she'd met him. She feared that gentleness and compassion had gone forever.

Her pulse increased, and her stomach lurched. Her first instinct was to run. She detested confrontations, they always ended the same way. Fighting back tears, she continued to stroke Balder's head, and desperately tried to maintain her composure in front of the servants.

"Happy Christmas, my lord." Her voice cracked with each word. Waving her hand toward the presents, she explained, "I was just handing out gifts to the staff."

"I can see that." Lord Hawthorne's tone was stern, harsh… cold. His eyes bore into her. The longer he stared at her, the more uncomfortable she felt. And then he strolled up to her, his tall form towering over her petite figure.

She wanted to run and hide. It was her fault that he was unhappy. It was her carelessness that had got them both into this situation.

The seconds ticked by. Faith hoped the floor would open up and swallow her whole. Perhaps then she would find some peace.

"Finish, and then I would like a word with you in my study."

All speech escaped her. She nodded in acquiescence and then turned to continue handing out the gifts. Dread sank further into the pit of her stomach, and her shoulders slumped in defeat. She had decorated Deer Park, hoping that her husband would spend Christmas at the house *and* be pleased with her efforts. Out of the corner of her eye, she watched him storm off. She took in a deep, jagged breath. *It will be alright.*

No one said a word now that the lively festive atmosphere had dissipated. All that remained was a dull silence, interrupted only by the sound of footsteps as servants came forth to receive their boxes.

By the time Faith presented the last gift, all efforts to maintain composure had failed. Her knees were wobbling and she could not contain the tremors that crept up her body. She detested the look of pity she saw in all their eyes. She did not want their sympathy, she wanted respect. But most of all, she wanted acceptance and love.

Troth cast a consoling look at her. Over the past months, the woman had become more than just a lady's maid, she'd become a trusted friend. She was the only person in the world who knew Faith's secret.

Sucking in a deep breath, Faith could no longer delay the inevitable. The time had come to face her husband.

A slow funeral march played over and over in her head as she walked toward her imminent doom. The walls inched closer about her with each step she took, and the fragrant evergreen air stifled her breathing. "It will be fine. He will not be like Father," she murmured to herself. Except for his temper, Lord Hawthorne had never given her cause to fear him. *Just like Father before Mary died.*

Shaking that thought from her mind, she smoothed the front of her dress with unsteady hands. Turning the corner, she gazed down the long, dark hall.

Weighed down with fear, she had to convince her legs to move forward. "It will be fine," she chanted softly to herself over and over.

She stopped and, standing frozen in place, stared at the dark mahogany door, debating her next course of action. For one brief moment, she thought to run in the opposite direction and find a safe hiding spot.

With one hand resting on the elegant brass knob, she tried to convince herself once again. *I can do this.* She closed her eyes, attempting to numb the feelings that were lashing through her body. "He is not Father," she murmured to herself. *He is not like Father.*

Marcus, the Marquess of Hawthorne, paced the length of the room for the umpteenth time. How dare she give gifts to *his* servants without his permission? Then his conscience reminded him they were now her servants too, but that was a whole other matter. He shook his head. And his dog had actually growled at him. The traitor had growled at *him*!

Running a hand through his hair, he scolded himself. *What the hell am I doing here?* He detested the effect his wife had on him. He had spent years avoiding such emotions, and in one evening, all his efforts had been thrown out of the carriage and trampled upon by a dozen horses.

After his hasty marriage four months ago, he'd hied his unwanted bride off to the country and returned to London, hoping his family would not discover what he had done. It had been two months since his last disastrous visit to Deer Park. He had tried to stay away, but for the life of him, he could not. He didn't want to *want* to see her. His unwanted wife may have been out of sight these past couple of months, but she was never far from his thoughts. How could she be?

The night they'd first met in London still haunted him. He had never been so attracted to a woman in his entire life. She had been wearing the same pale blue gown she wore tonight. He had barely been able to keep his wits about him then, and the effect had only worsened this evening. The blue gown deepened the color of her eyes, and her fair blonde hair shimmered like freshly fallen snow on a moonlight night. From the start, her sweet nature and bashful glances had mesmerized him.

It was all a lie, his heart chided. He should have known better. *Her father tricked you into marrying her,* he reminded himself. Every instinct told him she was just a victim, but his heart convinced him she could not be trusted.

Where is she? His patience was hanging by a thread.

He eyed the stack of responsibilities piled on his desk. He should not have neglected his duties for so long. Sifting through the correspondences, he tossed the ones that did not need his immediate attention aside, next to the small holly and ivy centerpiece. "What is keeping her?" he grumbled to himself. Patience was not one of his attributes.

Throwing the rest of the envelopes down, he marched to the door, grabbed the knob, and pulled the door open wide. A petite figure tumbled forward into his arms. The world stood still for a moment and vanilla enraptured his senses. His hands ached to explore, to claim what was his.

She pulled away with haste. A red blush stained her cheeks. "I apologize. I..."

"What took you so long?" The words came out more harshly than he intended. He turned his back on her, not wanting her to see that she had discomposed him, and strolled to his desk.

"I…I was handing out the gifts, and..." Her voice quavered, then died away.

Marcus took his seat and sucked in a deep breath. He needed to gain control of his emotions. "Who gave you the liberty to decorate *my* house, present gifts to *my* staff, and God knows what else?" His voice reverberated through the room and, with each word that bellowed from his mouth, his wife took a small step back.

What was she hiding? He was convinced something nefarious was going on in his home, behind his back.

"It is Christmastide and…" Her words trailed off and she began to worry her bottom lip.

He would not fall for that ploy. He would not succumb to any of her enticements. Narrowing his gaze on her, he waited for her to finish speaking.

The silence dragged out for several seconds before she continued. "I thought it would be a pleasant surprise." Her eyes were wet with unshed tears.

Don't fall for this charade. A woman's tears would not fool him again. Not ever again.

Her gaze shifted downward, and she stared at the rug, clasping the sides of her dress. When she finally looked up and spoke, her voice was soft and meek, almost unsure. "I…I was hoping you would be pleased and… I just wanted to celebrate Christmastide, my lord."

His temper reached a new height the moment she began to weep. How dare she come into his house and stir memories he'd buried deep into the recesses of his mind. She had even decorated his study!

His fists tightened. He wanted to hit something. Slamming his hand down on the desk with more force than he intended, he stood and walked around the desk. His wife flinched and closed her eyes. That behavior took him aback.

Lady Hawthorne, his wife only in name, stood with her eyes shut tight, a grimace encompassing her features. She was trembling from head to toe, swaying from side to side. Something was not quite right. Concern nibbled at his conscience.

Standing in front of her, he softened his tone. "Open your eyes." With her head still hung low, she did as he commanded. A stream of tears continued anew. She flinched again as he tucked his index finger under her chin.

When he raised her chin, she stared at him with questioning, almost terrified, eyes. He did not know what he was looking for, so he squinted and leaned in closer. Her scent was sweet and enticing, and her skin glowed against the soft candlelight.

Pulling away, she cried, "Please don't!" Before he could say a word, she ran to the door, flung it open, and scurried into the darkness.

Go after her.

His damn conscience should mind its own business!

Guilt pressed against his chest. Perhaps he had been too harsh. Running a frustrated hand through his hair, he walked with reluctance toward the door. Best to deal with this now.

He had only taken a couple of steps when Caspar entered, silver tray in hand. "This has just arrived for you, my lord. The young man said it was urgent and is waiting for an answer."

What, now? He had not even been home for half a day, and he was being bombarded with problems. He took the missive from the salver and tore it open. Pinching the bridge of his nose, he took in a deep breath.

Damn his cousin.

"Send him in."

AN HOUR later saw one scandal averted, and it was now time to deal with his wife. He didn't know what he was going to say yet, but he would do his best not to lose his temper... again. This place brought back too many childhood memories that he'd rather forget. He shook those distant thoughts away and summoned Caspar to the study.

"Fetch Lady Hawthorne. Tell her I wish to speak with her immediately."

Caspar did not question or look twice as he set about his task, while Marcus began to formulate in his head what he was going to say. Time and again, Faith had declared that she'd had no knowledge of her father's actions. Regardless, he needed to extract the truth before his aunt or grandmother discovered what he had done.

Twenty minutes ticked by and his mood did not improve. Lady Hawthorne was keeping him waiting for the second time in one evening. His rehearsed speech sounding, in his own mind, more like an interrogation than the conversation he was hoping to have.

At the sound of Caspar clearing his throat, he turned around. "She is nowhere to be found."

"It is ten o'clock at night. What do you mean, she is nowhere to be found?" The words rumbled past his lips.

"Troth said Lady Hawthorne returned to her room over an hour ago, visibly upset. She asked to be left alone." Caspar held out a scribbled note. "Troth found this on the bed."

Marcus grabbed the letter from Caspar. The two words jumped off the page and punched him in the gut.

I'm sorry.

Why would she apologize and then leave? Those two words echoed in his head. Had he really been that cruel to her? The events of the evening, the one-sided argument, and his reaction to her thoughtfulness toward the servants all spun through his mind, confusing his already muddled thoughts. *I'm sorry.* He had heard those words before from another woman who'd broken his heart over twenty years ago. He didn't know what to believe.

He walked to the window. The full moon illuminated the slumbering landscape and the coldness of winter emanated through the glass. Dark clouds had begun to roll in, consuming the night stars. She wouldn't dare venture out on a night like this, would she?

One thing was for certain, he could not live with himself if something should happen to her. Despite the way everything had happened between them, he was still responsible for her.

And you care for her.

He shook that thought away. "Gather the men together. I want her found tonight."

∾

Book Four in *A Waltz with Destiny* Series…
Dancing Around the Truth

ABOUT THE AUTHOR

Bestselling, award-winning author, Alanna Lucas pens Regency-set historicals filled with romance, adventure, and of course, happily ever afters. When she is not daydreaming of her next travel destination, Alanna can be found researching, spending time with family, volunteering, or going for long walks. She makes her home in California with her husband, children, one sweet dog, and hundreds of books.

Just for the record, you can never have too many handbags or books. And travel is a must.

ALSO BY ALANNA LUCAS

Mistletoe Waltz

A Waltz with Destiny: Book Three

Dancing into the arms of love?

Marcus, Lord Hawthorne, vowed never to fall in love, the past having taught him that marriage can only ever lead to heartbreak. So, how has he allowed himself to be tricked into being leg-shackled to Faith Whitworth, the daughter of a scheming businessman who wants entry to the *ton*?

Marcus's solution for dealing with his unwanted wife is to keep her at Deer Park, his country estate, while he stays in London. But when he returns at Christmastime, he is surprised to find that not only does Faith revel in her role as his marchioness, she is sweet and lovely—and he desires her. This was never part of his plan. However, the arrival of relatives means he won't be able to escape until the yuletide festivities are over.

As Twelfth Night approaches, Faith's gentleness and beauty are growing on Marcus more and more. He realizes he wants to dance with her forever, in a marriage that's more than in name only. He knows he can protect her from her ruthless papa and make her happy—just as long as he doesn't have to give her his heart…

Dancing Around the Truth

A Waltz with Destiny: Book Four

Mrs. Philippa Keates thought she'd found her happily ever after when she eloped, but two years later, she's named a widow. The horror of her husband's death, and then the shock of discovering that Alfred was a dissolute gambler, has forced Philippa into a life of seclusion. But when she is paid a visit by a woman claiming to be her late husband's wife and demanding recompense, Philippa knows she must emerge from mourning and discover the whole truth about Alfred. The one person who can assist her is her childhood friend, Benjamin Weston, for whom she once held a *tendre* until she realized he didn't feel the same.

Benjamin Weston, the illegitimate son of the late Baron Albryght, has made a name for himself conducting investigations for those willing to pay a high price for discretion. When Philippa arrives on his doorstep, begging for his assistance, Weston fears most of all that she will discover the truth. He insists that his investigations will be done on his terms, vowing to himself that he will continue to keep his distance from Philippa. But as he unravels her mystery, secrets of his own begin to come to light, and soon it becomes clear that there is more at stake than just Philippa's reputation.

Printed in Great Britain
by Amazon